AND
BEA
IT'S OWL GOOD

Meet Ollie and Bea.

(They don't know it yet, but they are
about to become best friends.)

RENÉE TREML

PICTURE WINDOW BOOKS
a capstone imprint

Published by Picture Window Books, an imprint of Capstone.
1710 Roe Crest Drive, North Mankato, Minnesota 56003
capstonepub.com

Text and illustrations copyright © 2022 by Renée Treml.

Library of Congress Cataloging-in-Publication Data
Names: Treml, Renée, author, illustrator.
Title: It's owl good / Renée Treml.
Other titles: It is owl good
Description: North Mankato, Minnesota : Picture Window Books, a Capstone
    imprint, [2022] | Series: The super adventures of Ollie and Bea | Audience: Ages
    5-7. | Audience: Grades K-1. | Summary: Ollie is an owl who wears glasses; Bea
    is a bunny with very big feet, and both are very self-conscious about what they
    see as flaws—but when they meet they help each other turn what seems at first
    to be problems into superpowers, and so become good friends.
Identifiers: LCCN 2021028669 (print) | LCCN 2021028670 (ebook) | ISBN
    9781663977175 (hardcover) | ISBN 9781666330847 (paperback) | ISBN
    9781666330854 (eBook pdf) | ISBN 9781666330878 (kindle edition)
Subjects: LCSH: Owls—Comic books, strips, etc. | Owls—Juvenile fiction. |
    Rabbits—Comic books, strips, etc. | Rabbits—Juvenile fiction. | Self-
    consciousness (Sensitivity)—Comic books, strips, etc. | Self-consciousness
    (Sensitivity)—Juvenile fiction. | Friendship—Comic books, strips, etc. |
    Friendship—Juvenile fiction. | Graphic novels. | Humorous stories. | CYAC:
    Graphic novels. | Owls—Fiction. | Rabbits—Fiction. | Self-consciousness
    (Sensitivity)—Fiction. | Friendship—Fiction. | Humorous stories. | LCGFT:
    Graphic novels. | Humorous fiction.
Classification: LCC PZ7.7.T73 It 2022 (print) | LCC PZ7.7.T73 (ebook) | DDC
    741.5/994—dc23
LC record available at https://lccn.loc.gov/2021028669
LC ebook record available at https://lccn.loc.gov/2021028670

Designed by Kay Fraser

Printed and bound in the USA. 4608

TABLE OF CONTENTS

CHAPTER 1

OH, *DEER!*

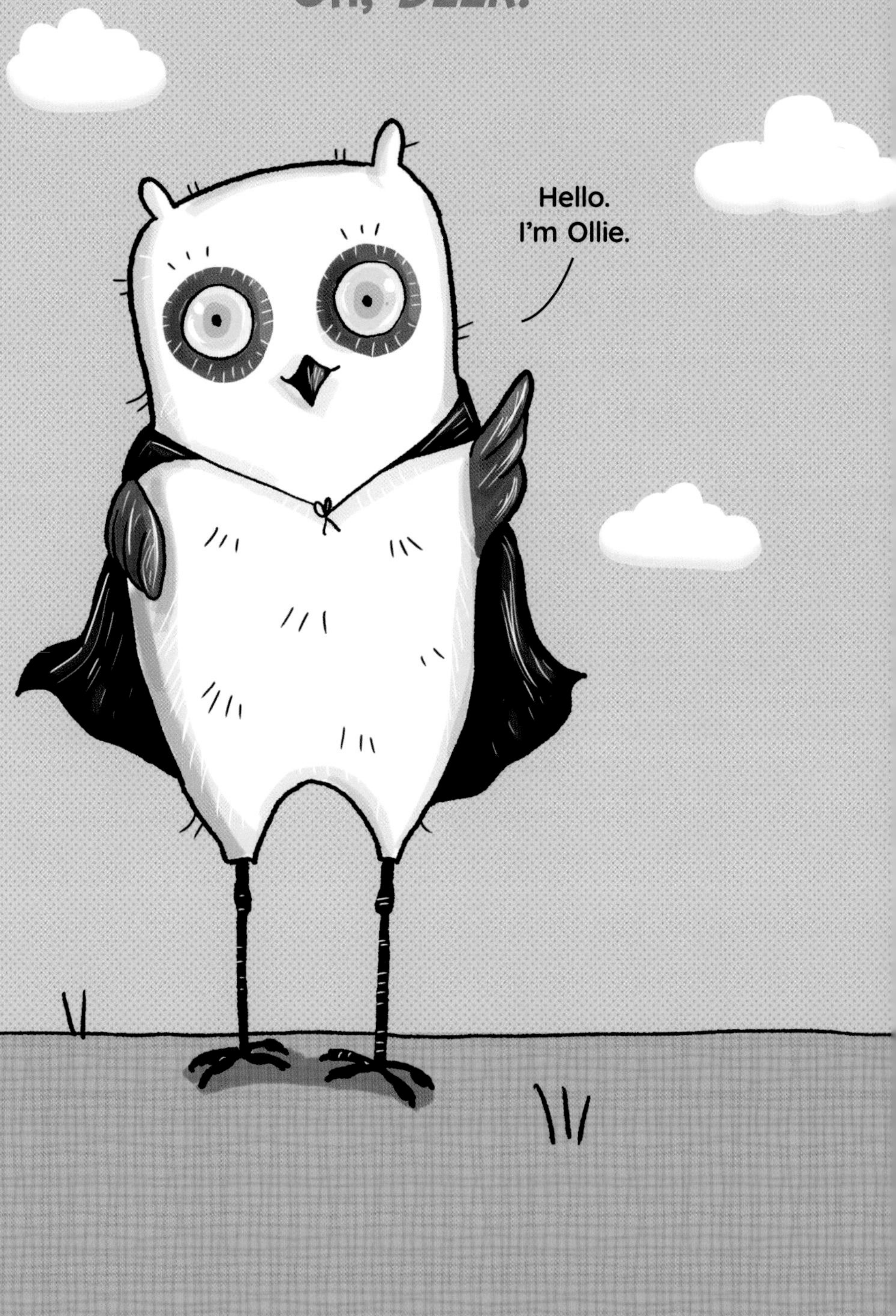
Hello.
I'm Ollie.

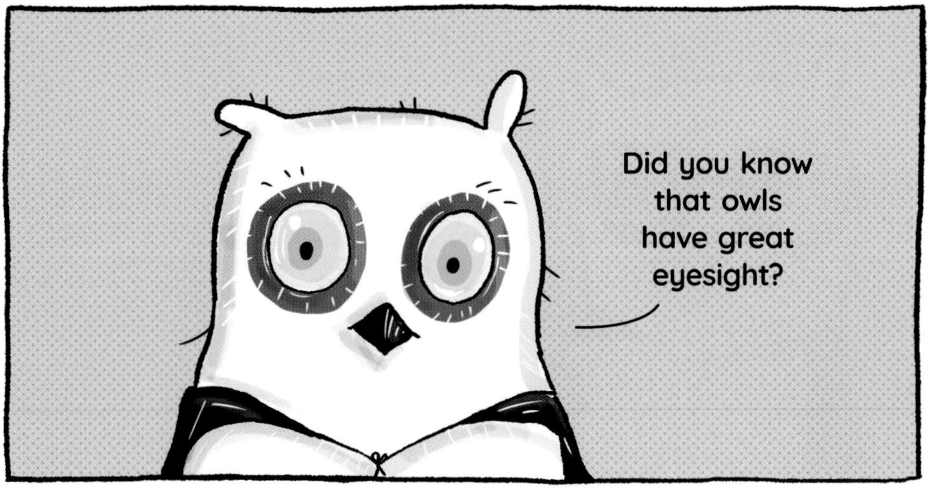
Did you know that owls have great eyesight?

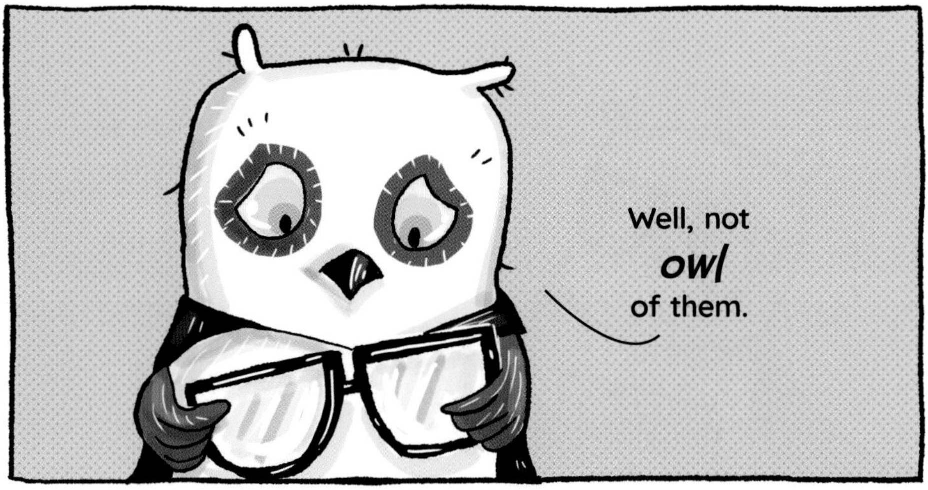
Well, not *owl* of them.

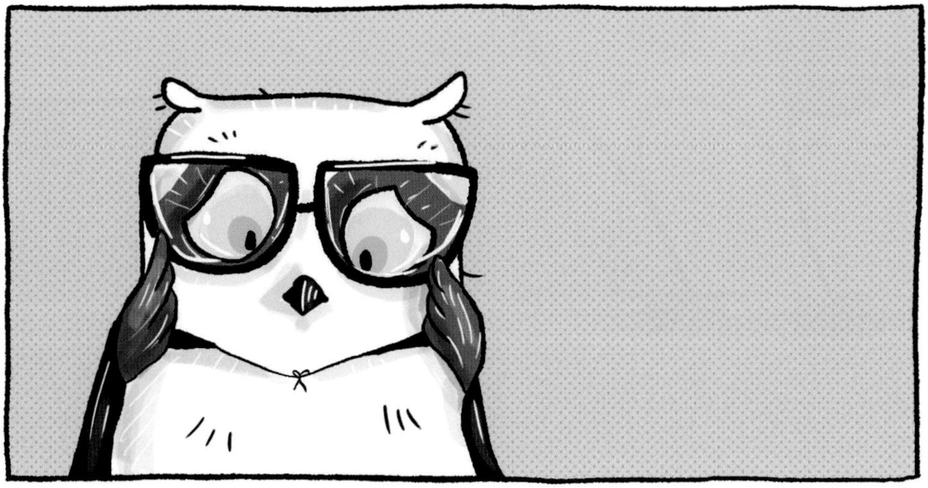

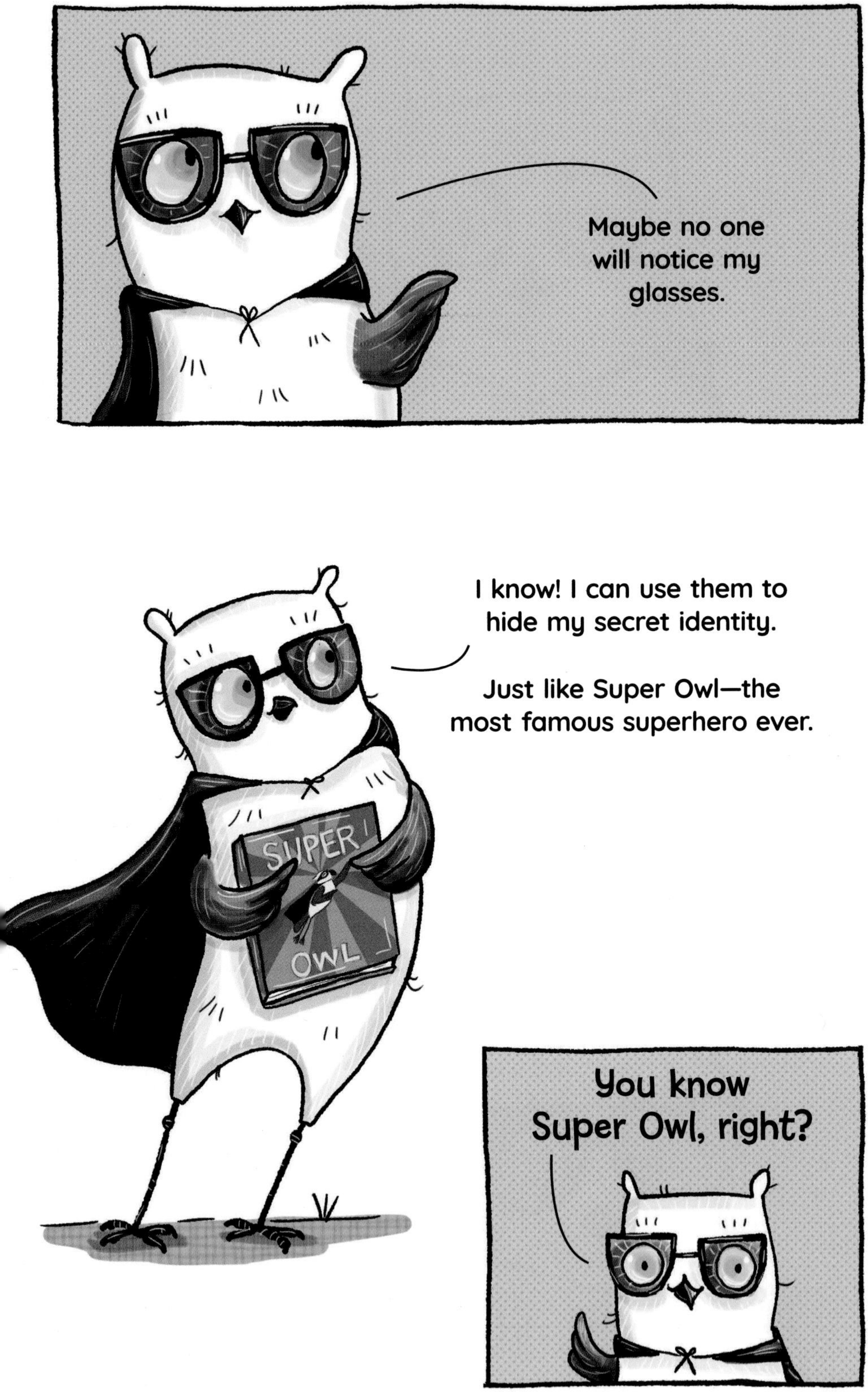
Maybe no one will notice my glasses.
I know! I can use them to hide my secret identity.
Just like Super Owl—the most famous superhero ever.
SUPER OWL
You know Super Owl, right?

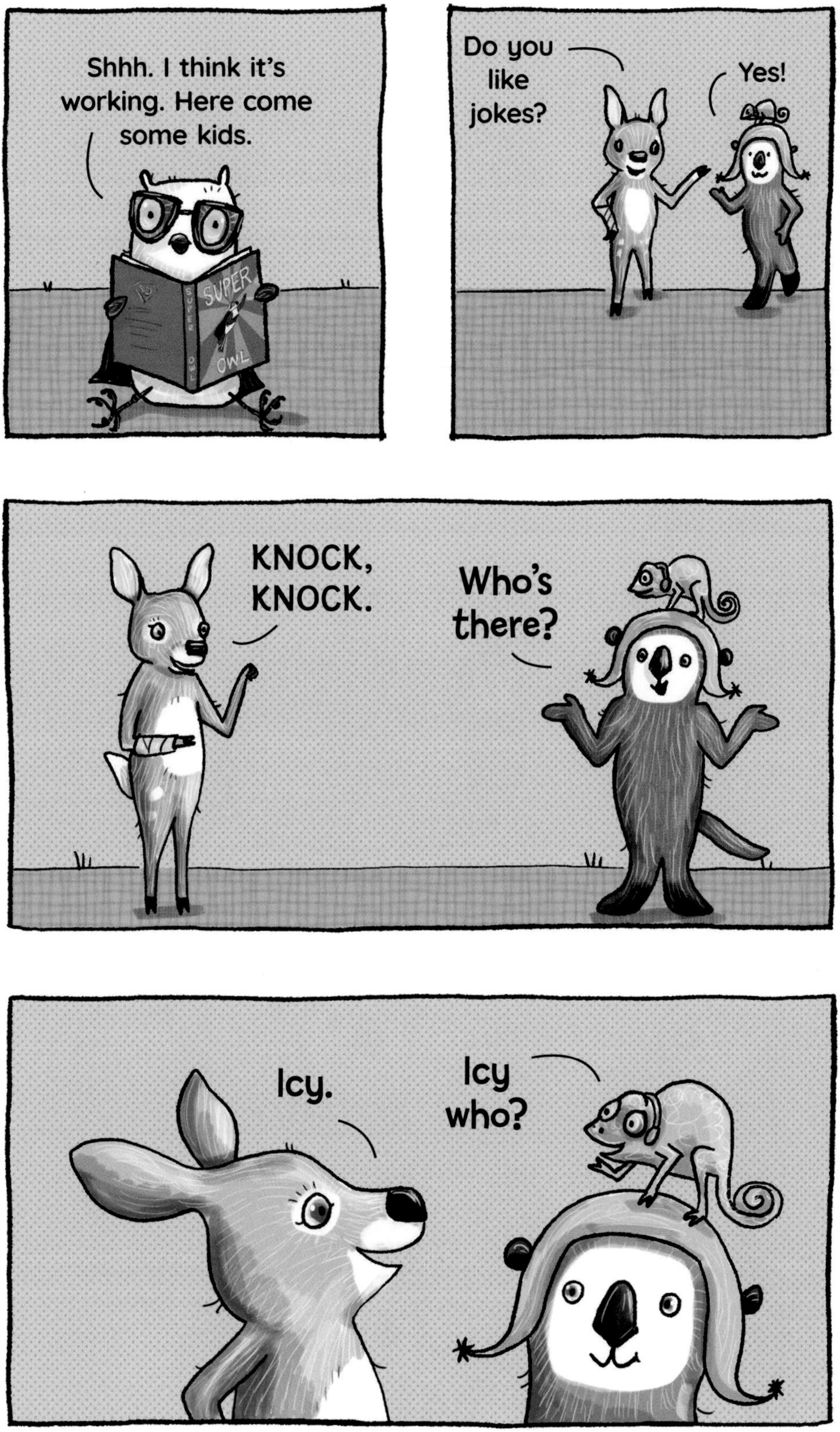
Shhh. I think it's working. Here come some kids.
SUPER OWL
Do you like jokes?
Yes!
KNOCK, KNOCK.
Who's there?
Icy.
Icy who?

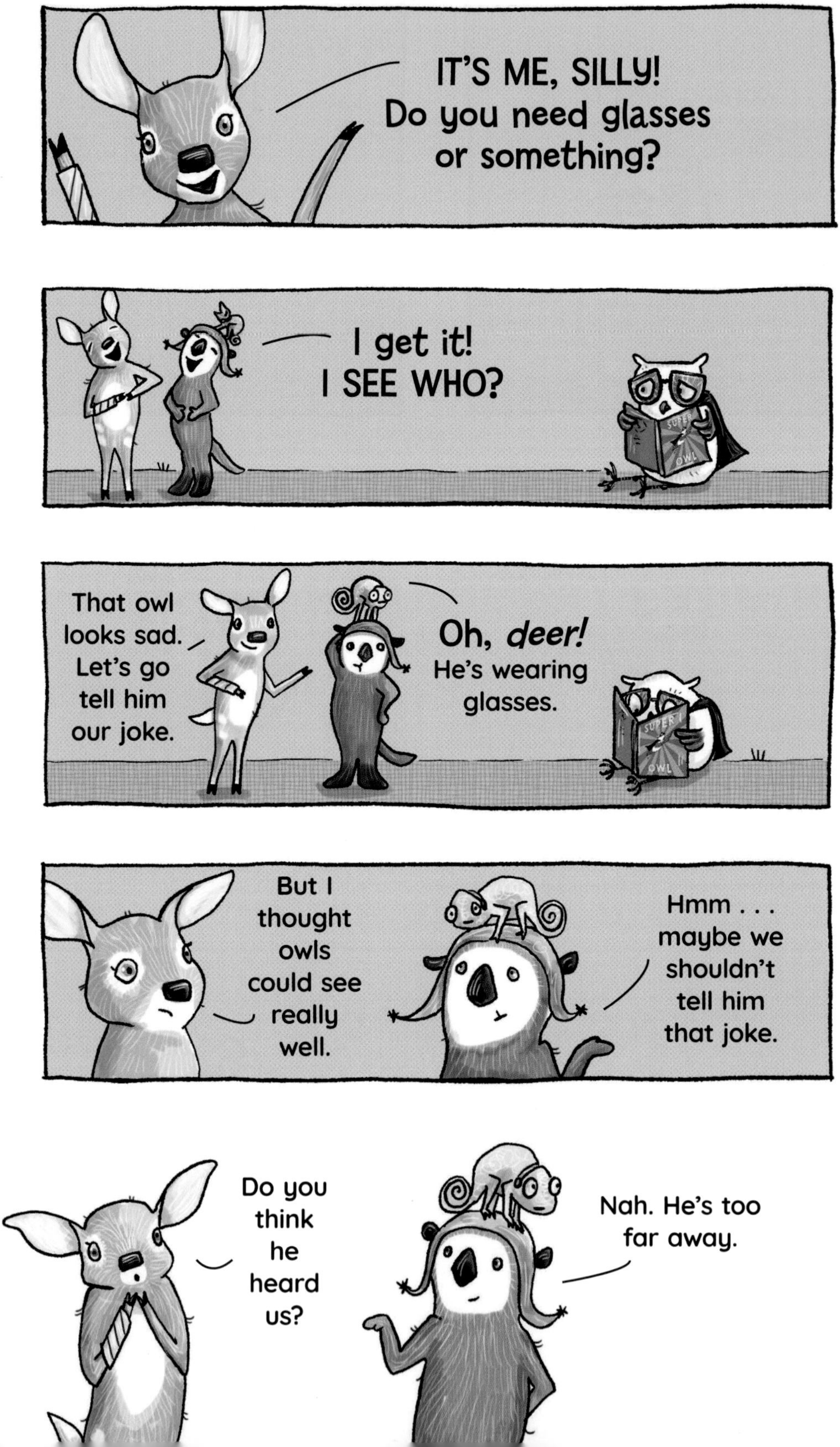
IT'S ME, SILLY!
Do you need glasses or something?
I get it!
I SEE WHO?
SUPER OWL
That owl looks sad. Let's go tell him our joke.
Oh, *deer!* He's wearing glasses.
SUPER OWL
But I thought owls could see really well.
Hmm . . . maybe we shouldn't tell him that joke.
Do you think he heard us?
Nah. He's too far away.

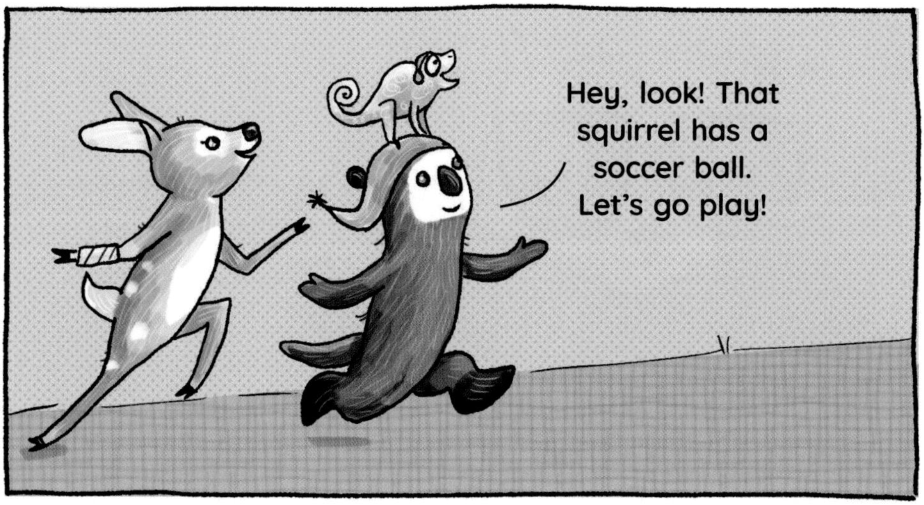
Hey, look! That squirrel has a soccer ball. Let's go play!

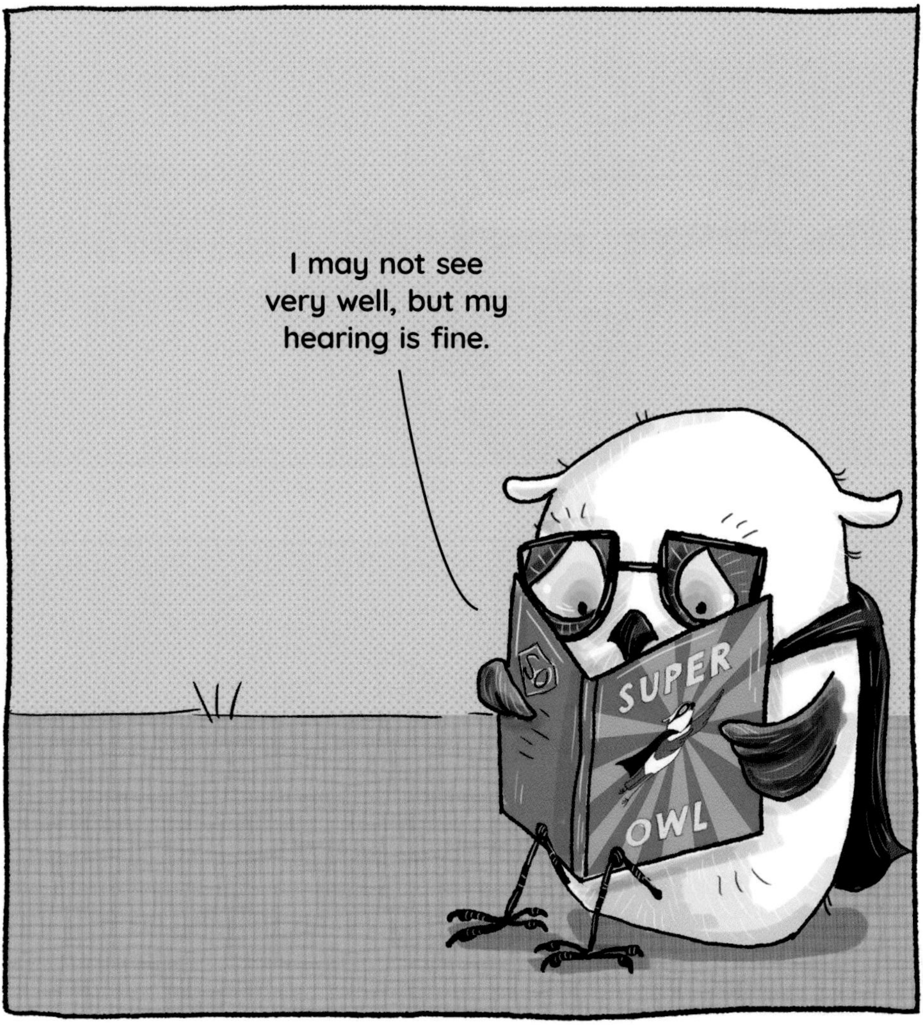
I may not see very well, but my hearing is fine.
SUPER
OWL

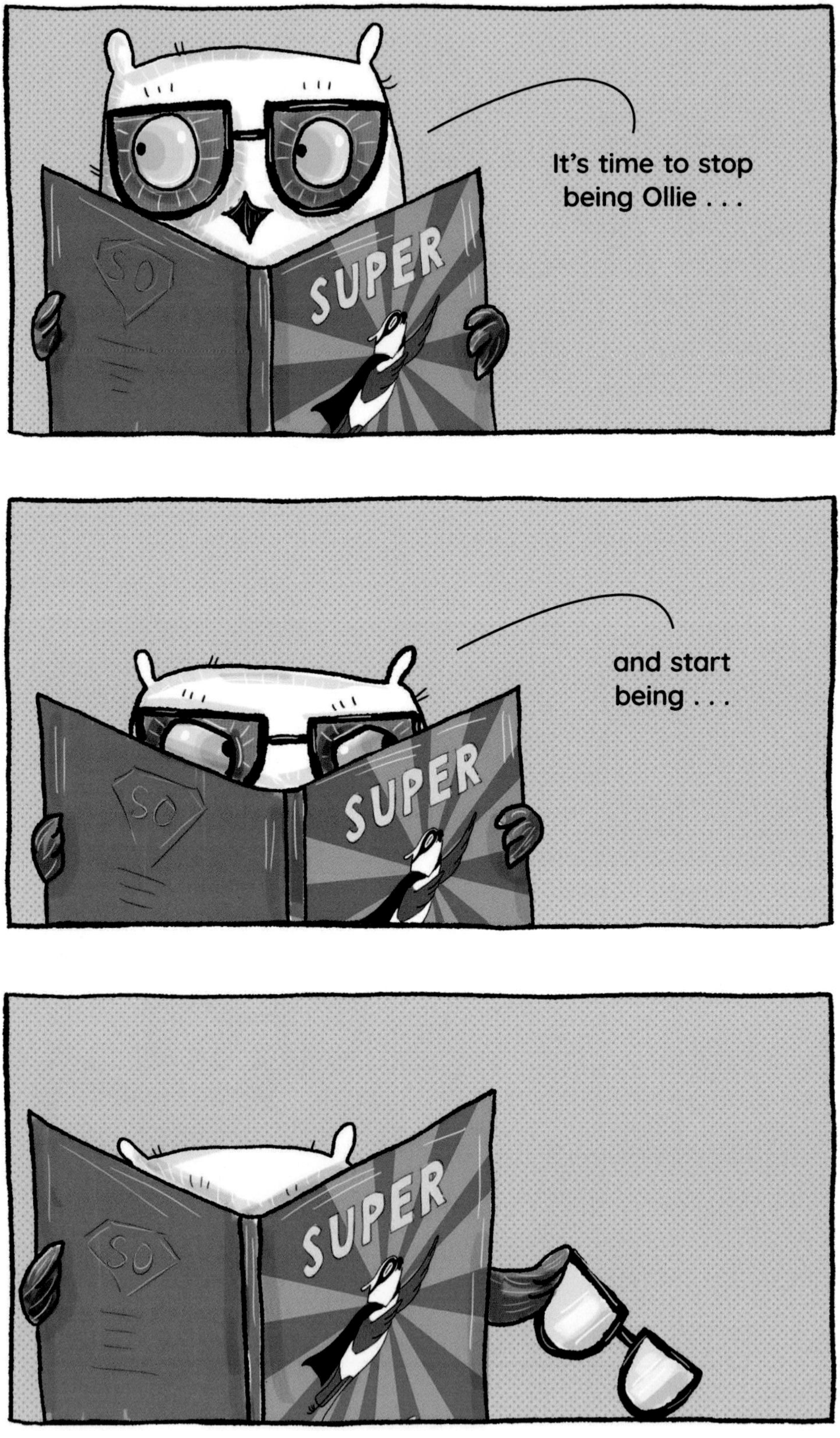
It's time to stop being Ollie . . .
and start being . . .
SUPER
SO

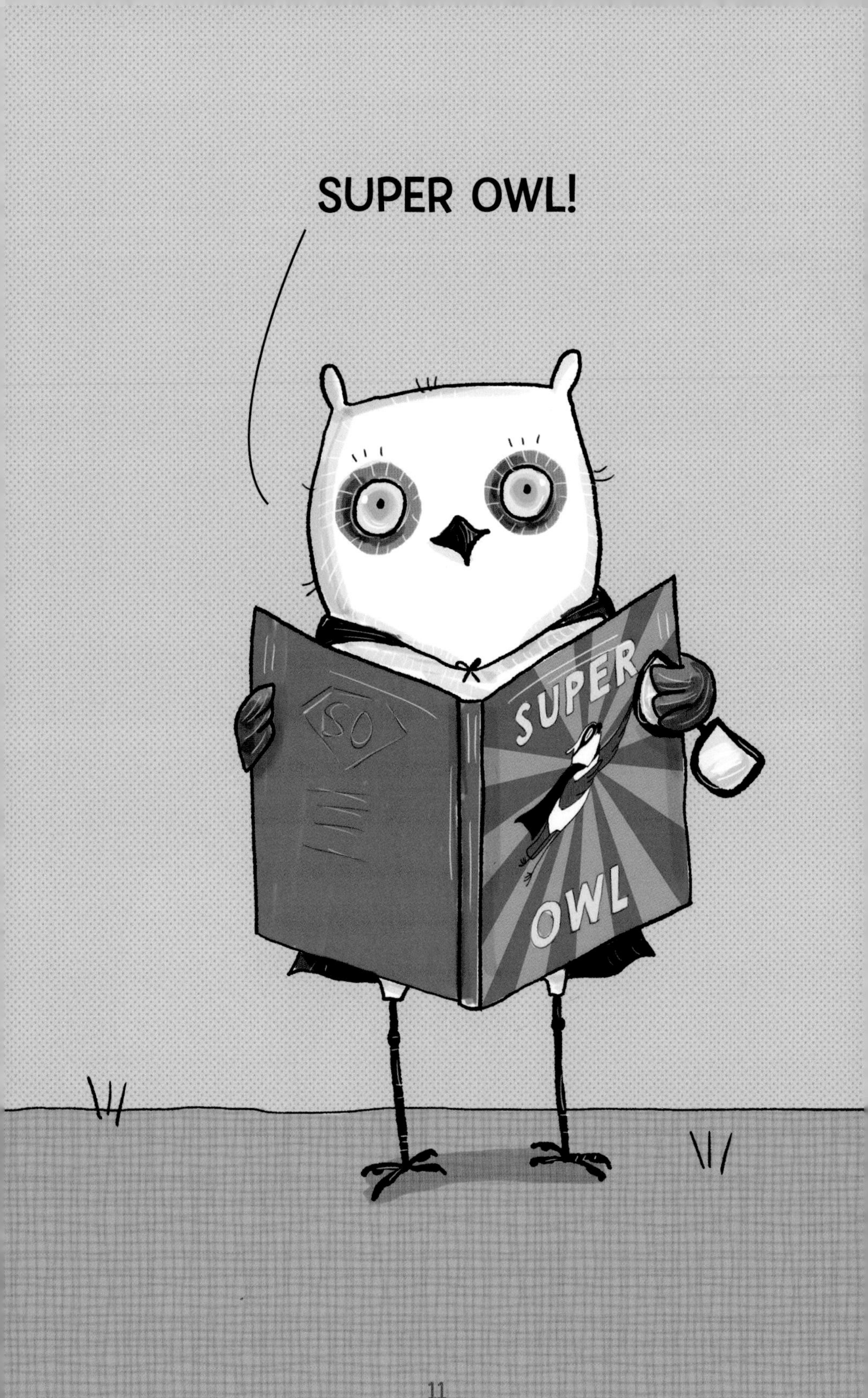
SUPER OWL!
SO
SUPER
OWL

CHAPTER 2

OWL BE SEEING YOU

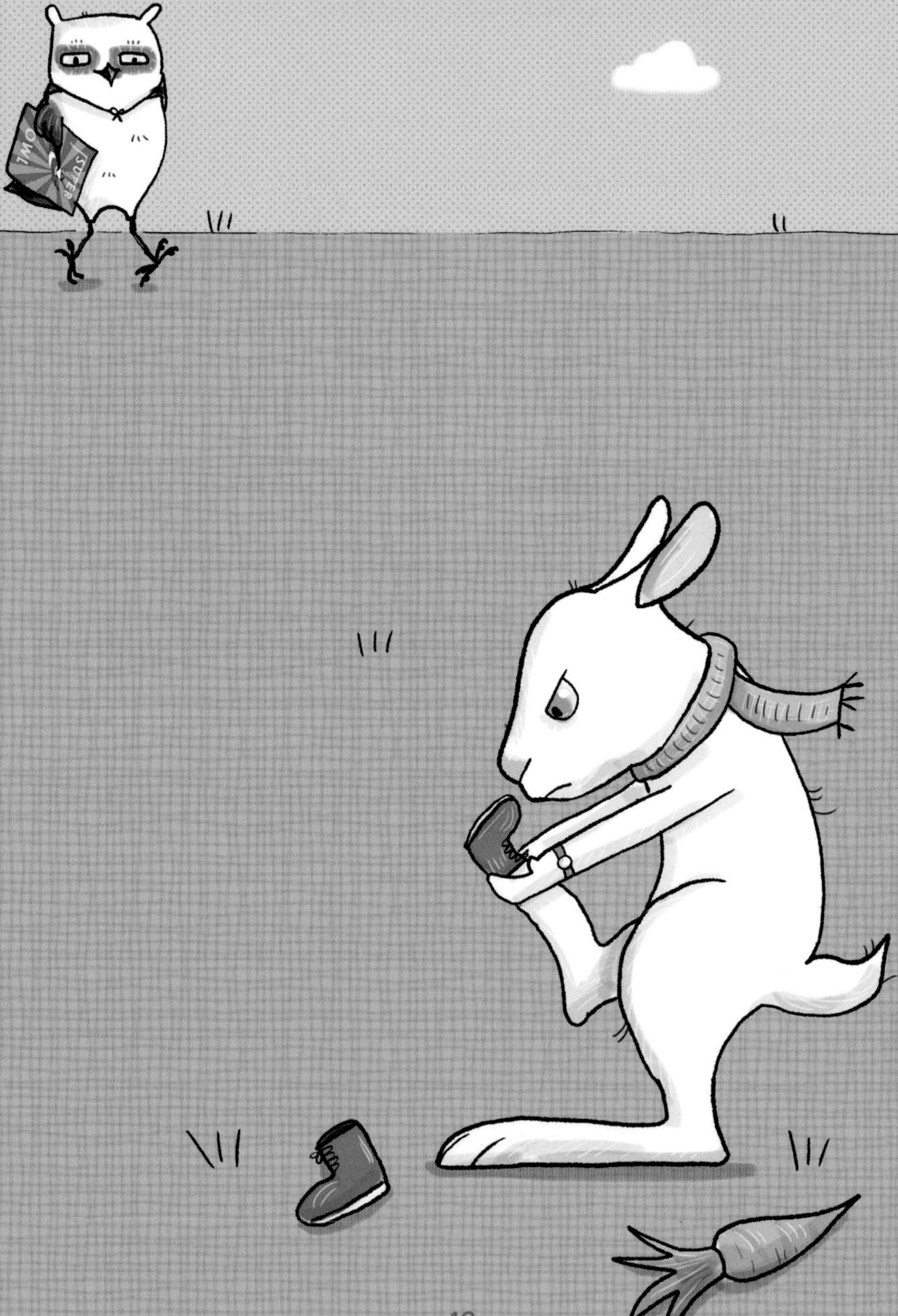
OWL
STUFF

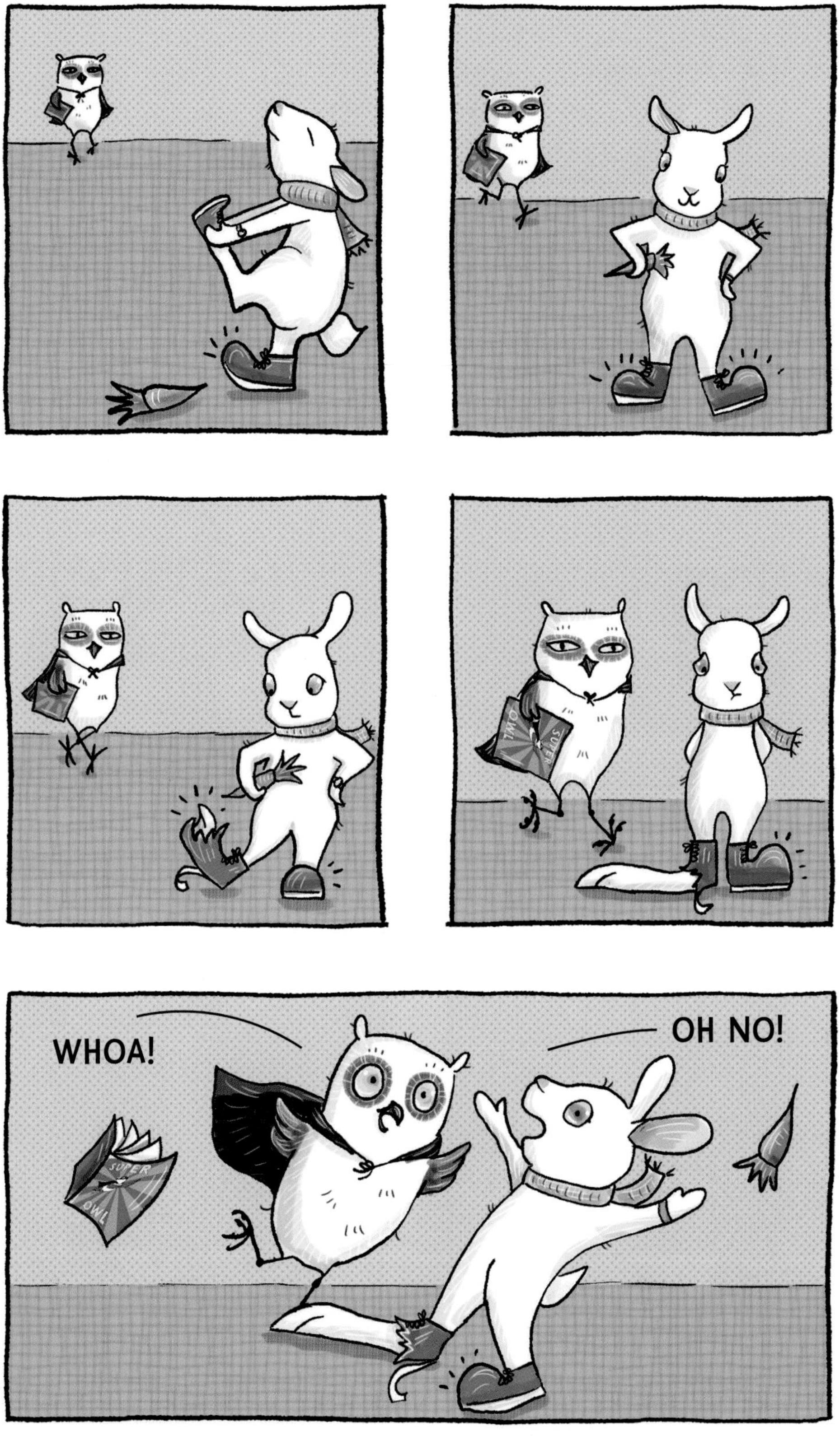
SUPER OWL
WHOA!
OH NO!
SUPER OWL

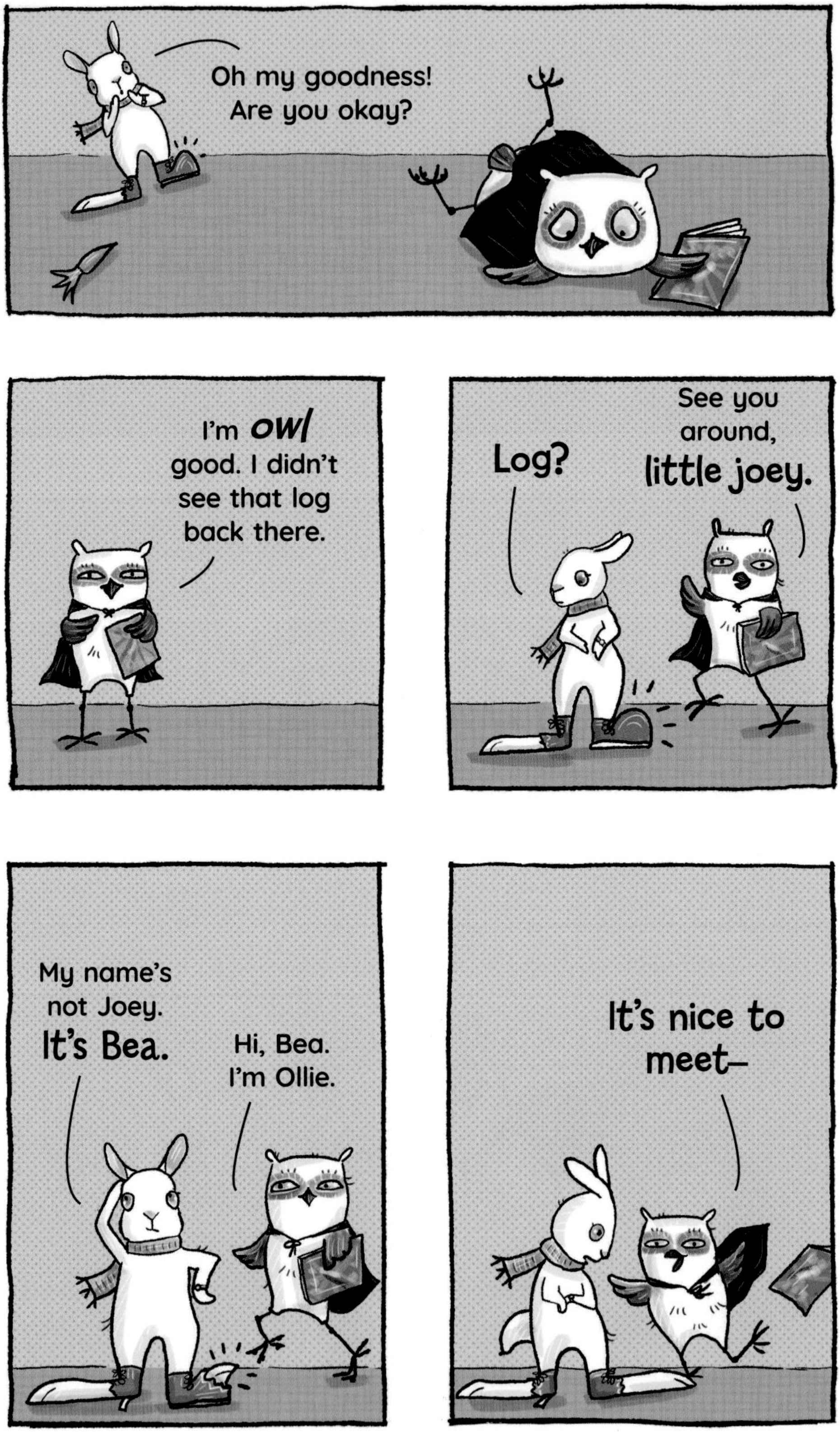
Oh my goodness! Are you okay?
I'm OWL good. I didn't see that log back there.
Log?
See you around, little joey.
My name's not Joey. It's Bea.
Hi, Bea. I'm Ollie.
It's nice to meet–

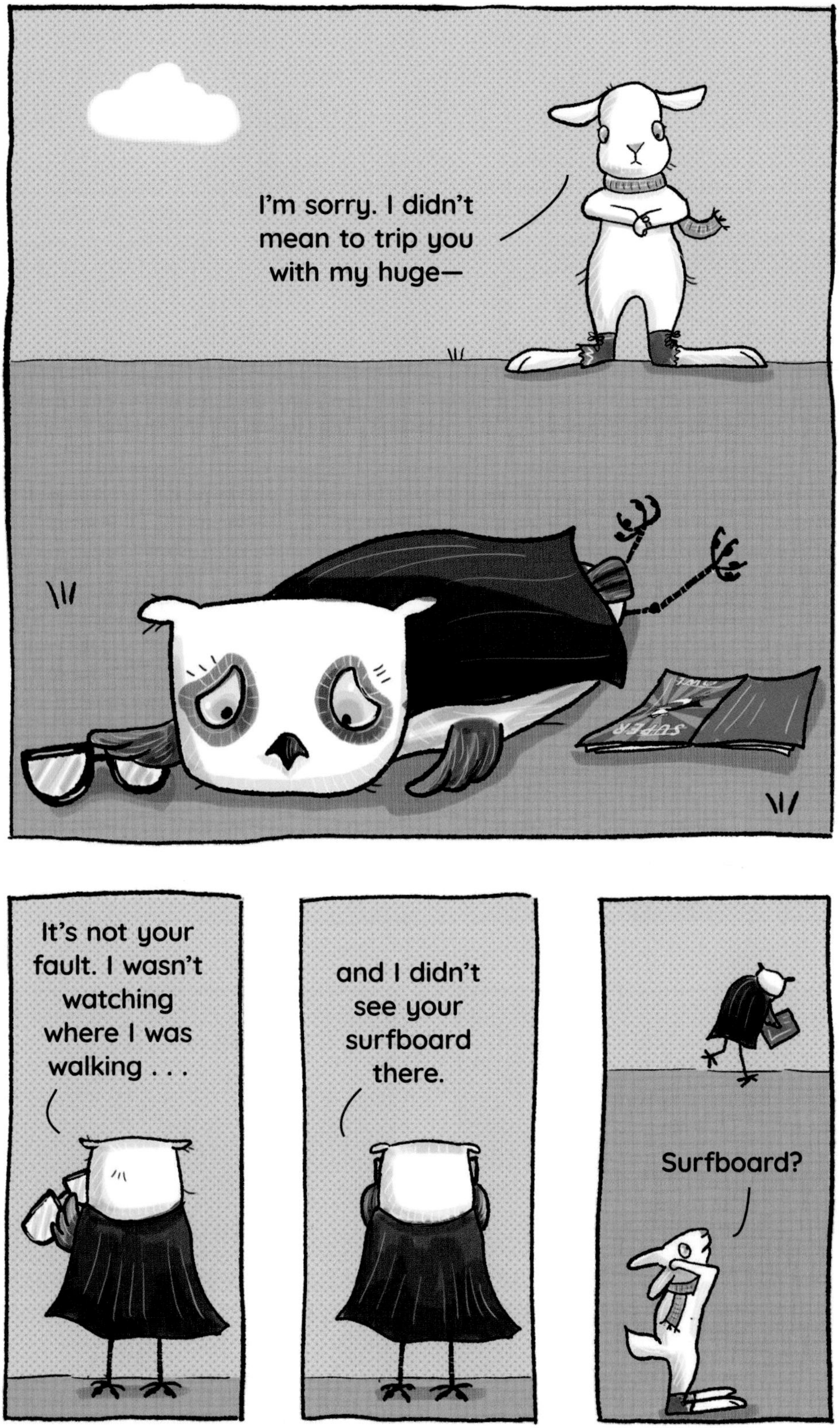
I'm sorry. I didn't mean to trip you with my huge—
It's not your fault. I wasn't watching where I was walking . . .
and I didn't see your surfboard there.
Surfboard?

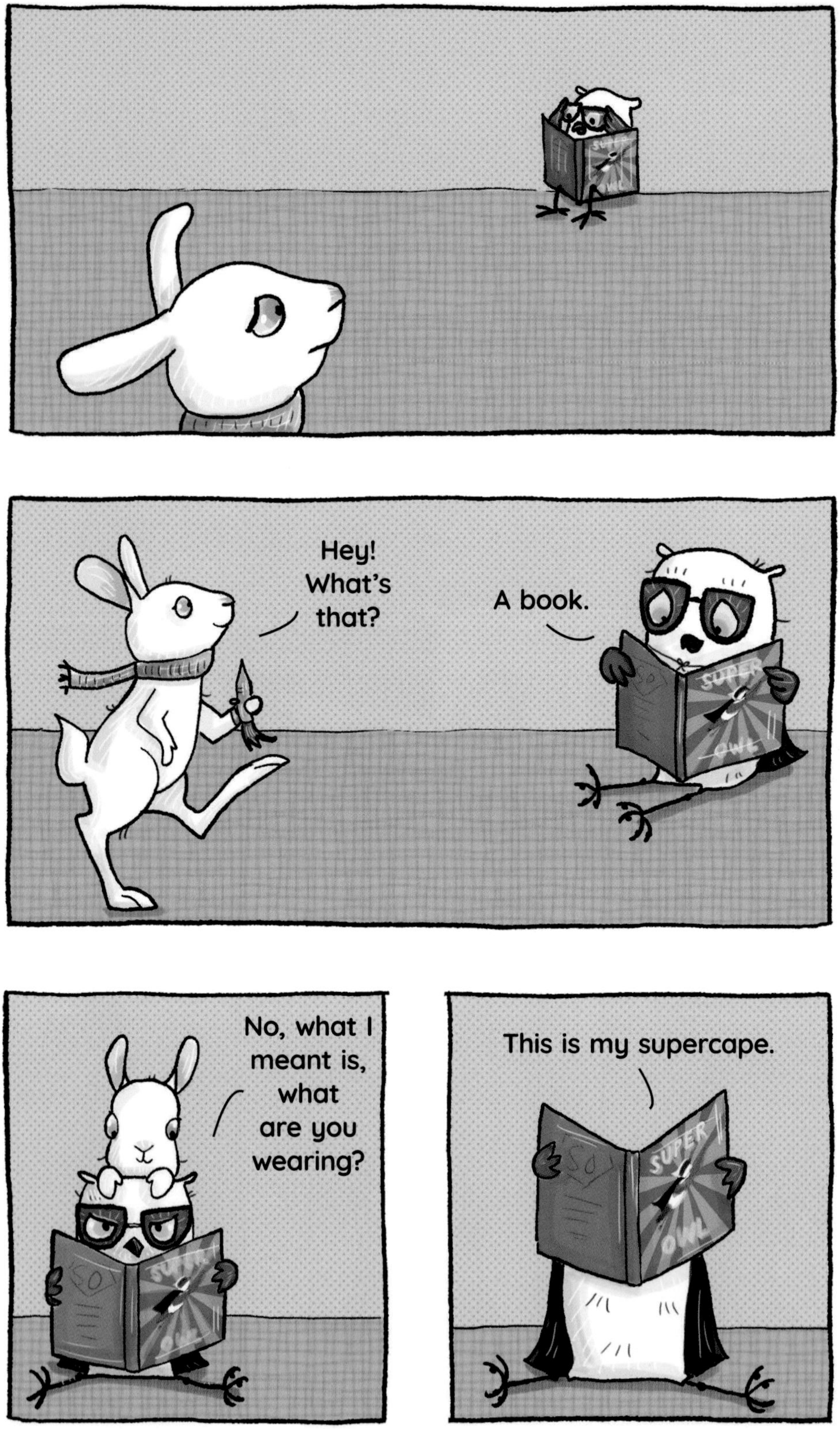
Hey! What's that?
A book.
No, what I meant is, what are you wearing?
This is my supercape.

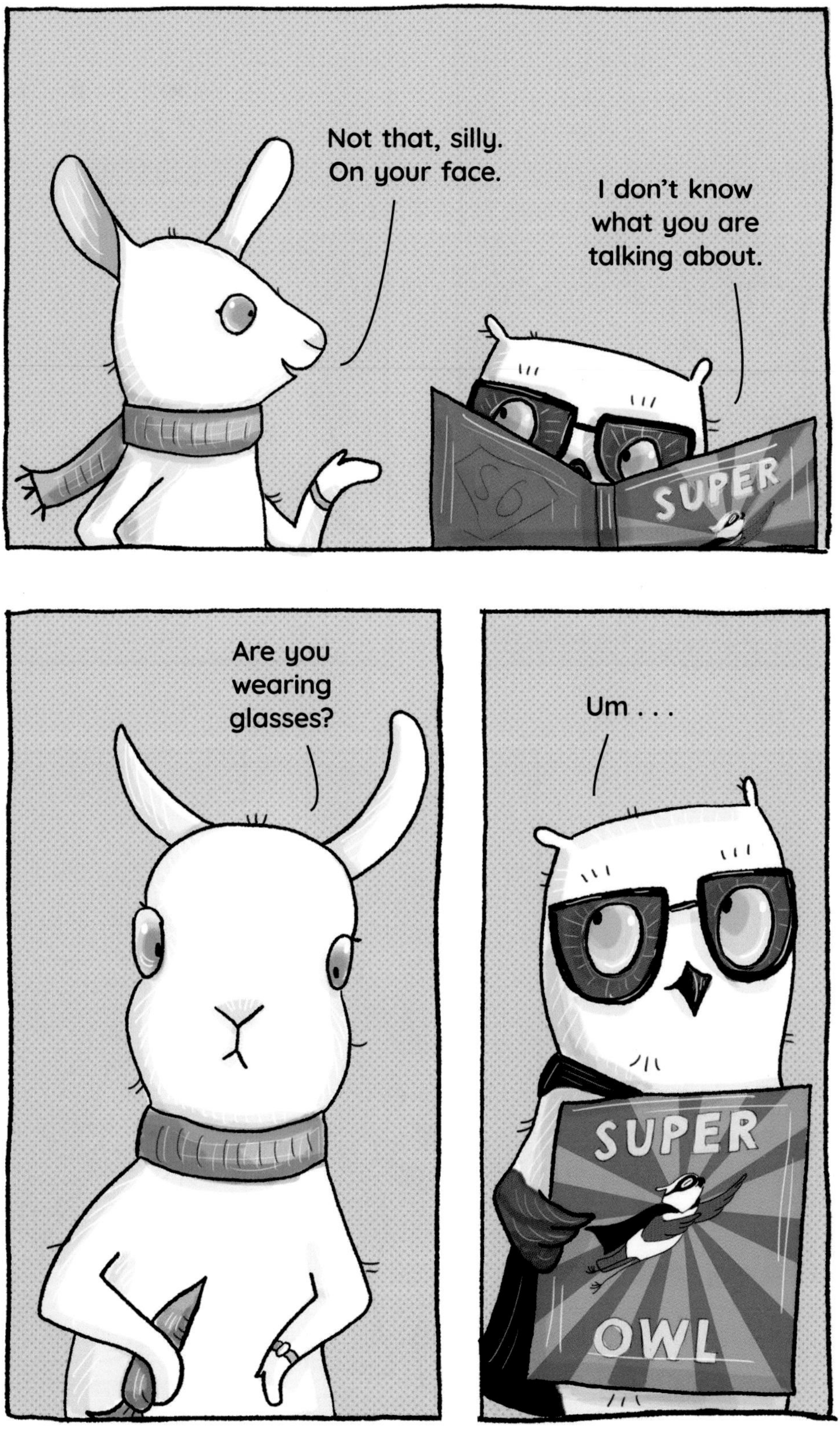
Not that, silly. On your face.
I don't know what you are talking about.
SUPER
Are you wearing glasses?
Um . . .
SUPER
OWL

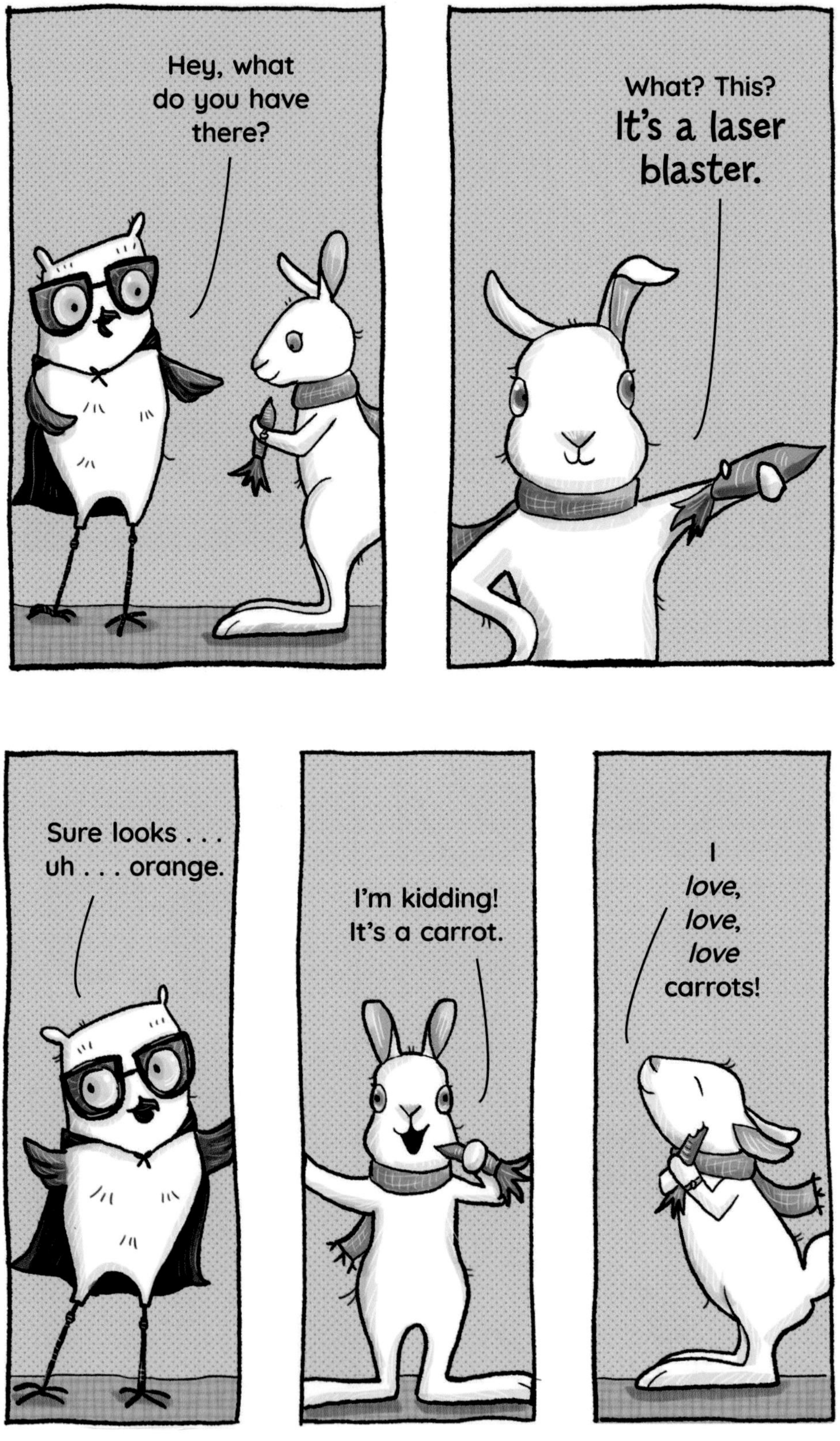
Hey, what do you have there?
What? This?
It's a laser blaster.
Sure looks . . . uh . . . orange.
I'm kidding! It's a carrot.
I *love, love, love* carrots!

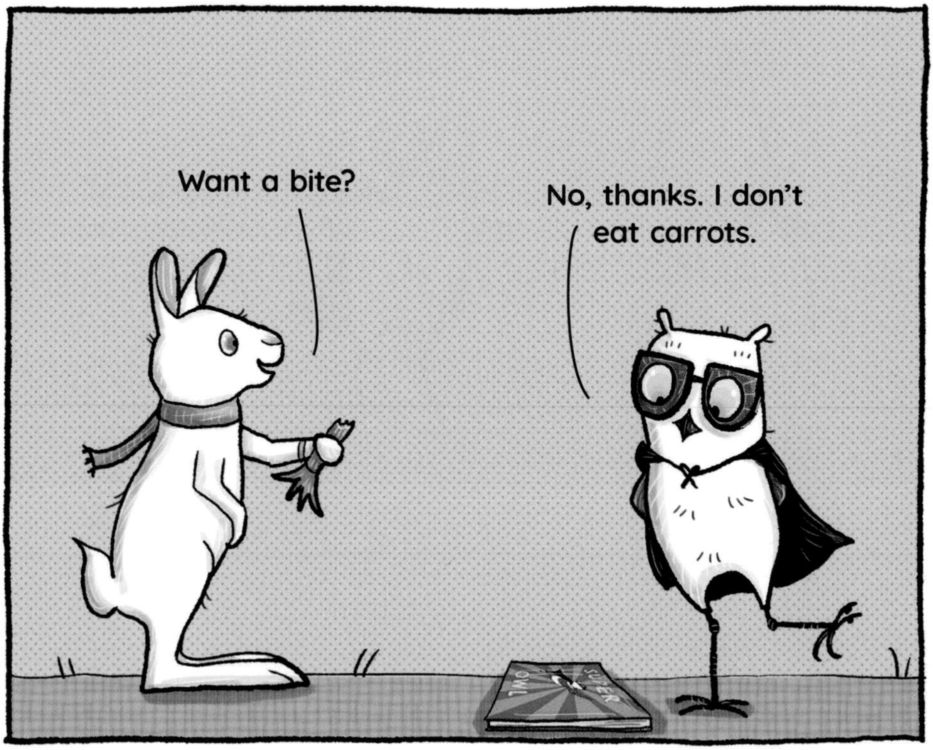
Want a bite?
No, thanks. I don't eat carrots.

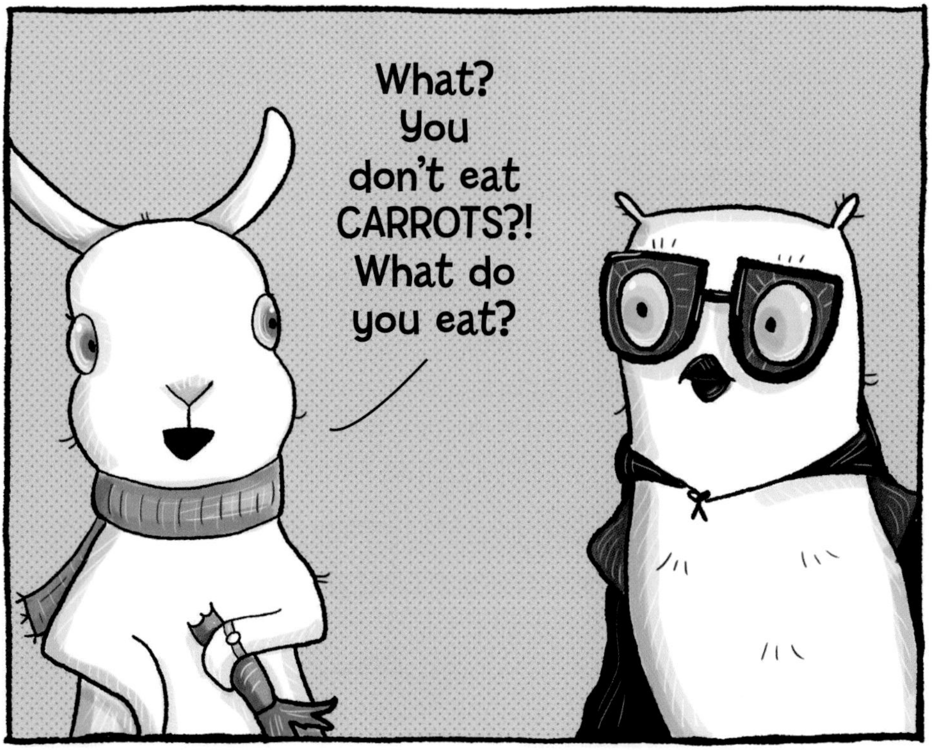
What? You don't eat CARROTS?! What do you eat?

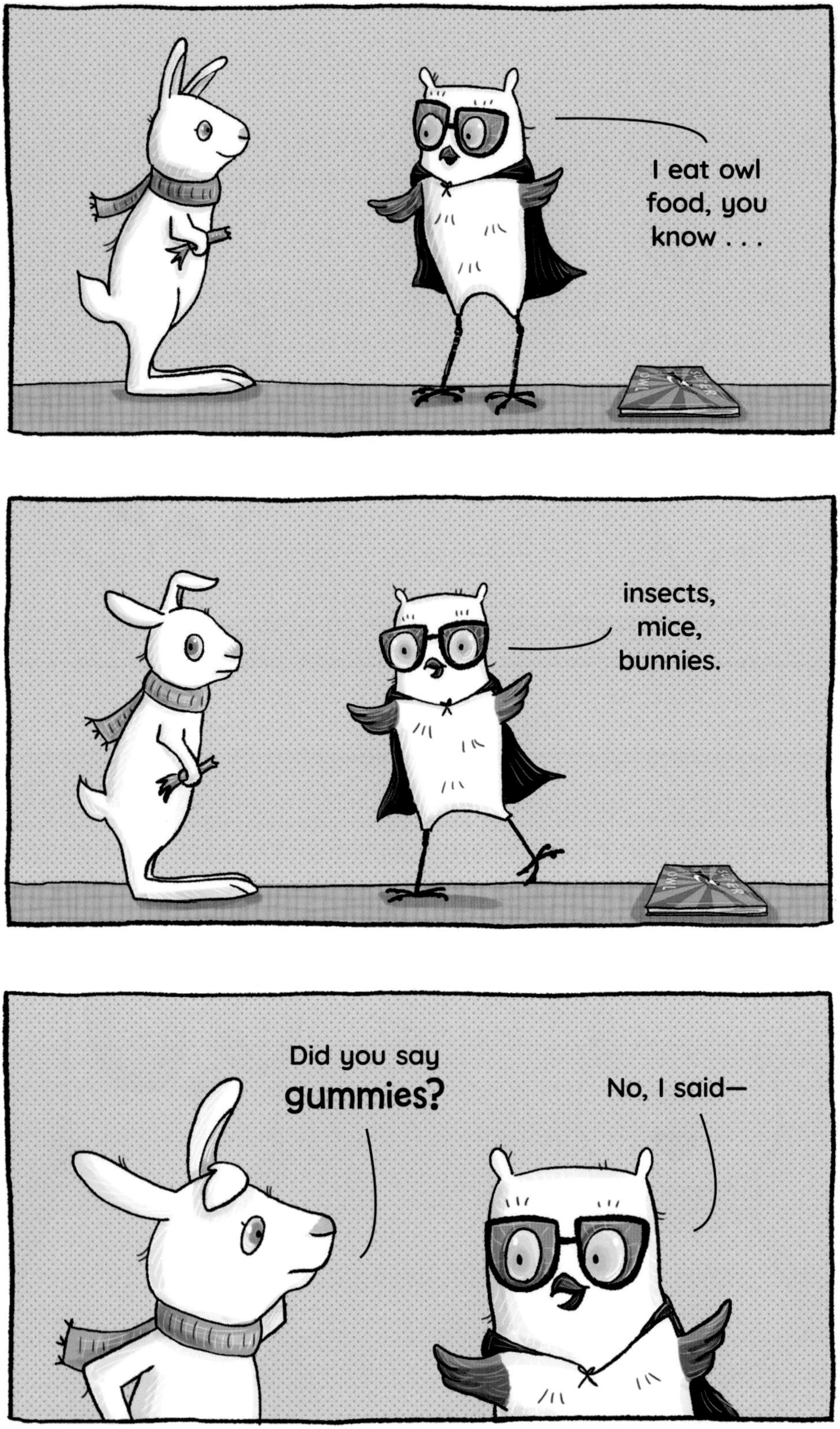
I eat owl food, you know . . .
insects, mice, bunnies.
Did you say **gummies?**
No, I said—

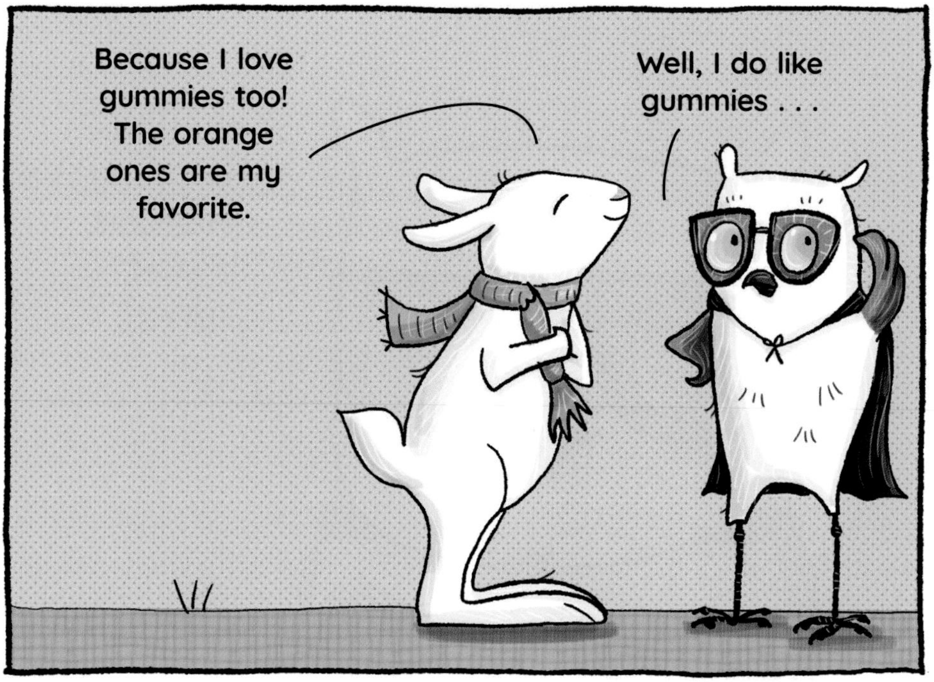
Because I love gummies too! The orange ones are my favorite.
Well, I do like gummies . . .

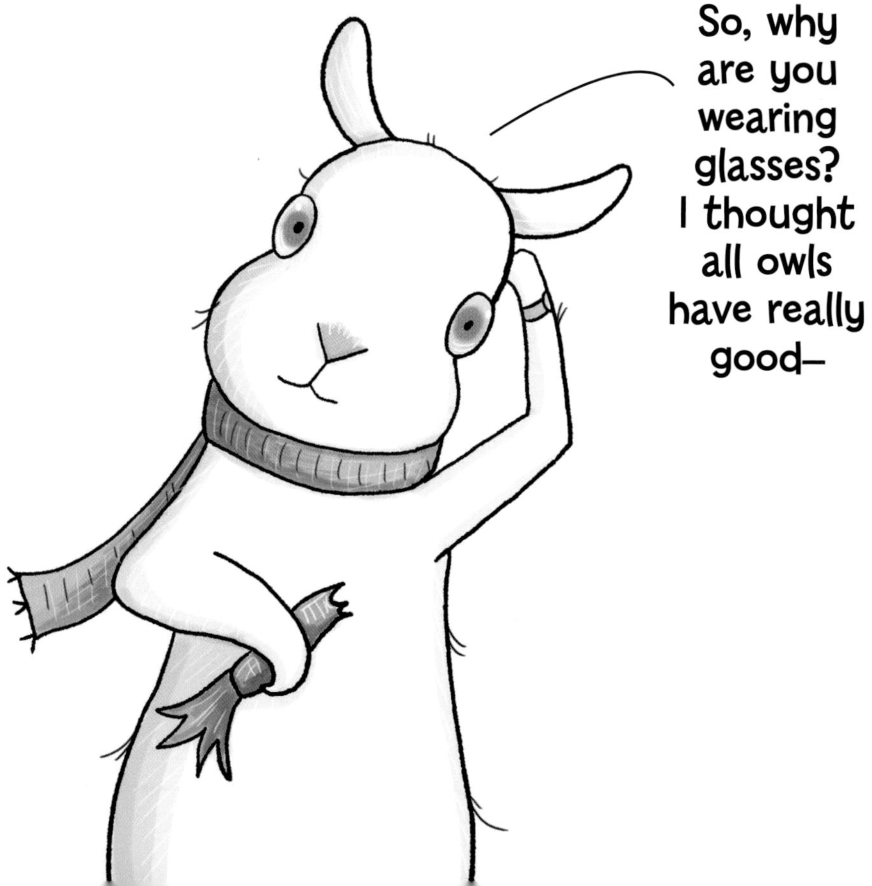
So, why are you wearing glasses? I thought all owls have really good–

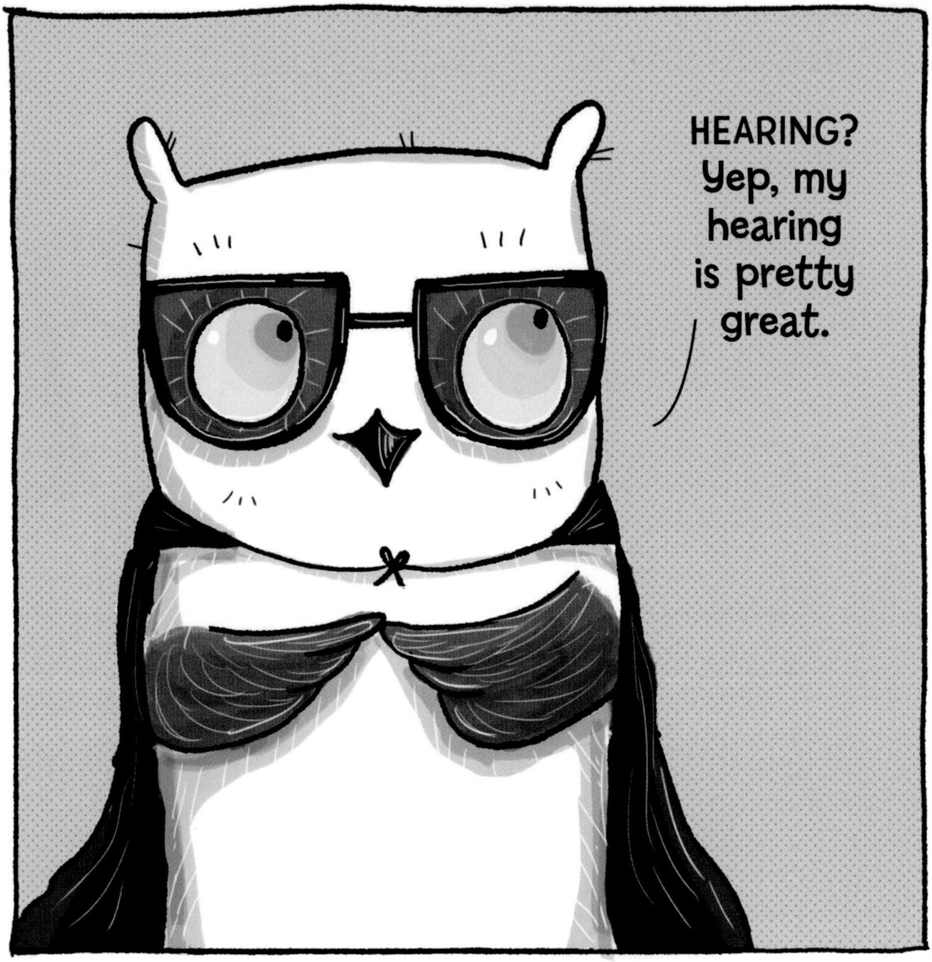
HEARING? Yep, my hearing is pretty great.

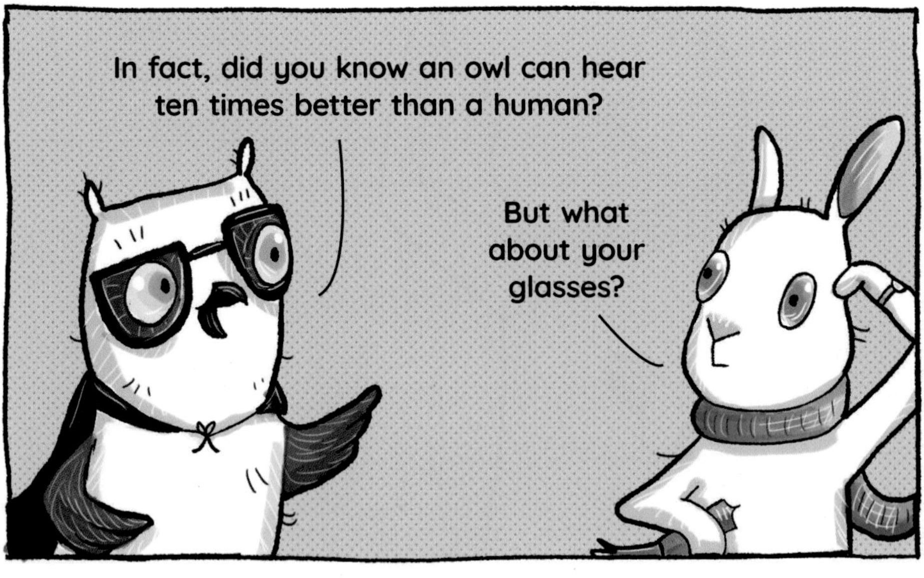
In fact, did you know an owl can hear ten times better than a human?
But what about your glasses?

My glasses are for . . .

well, actually . . .

about that . . .

they are . . .

you know . . .

I can't—

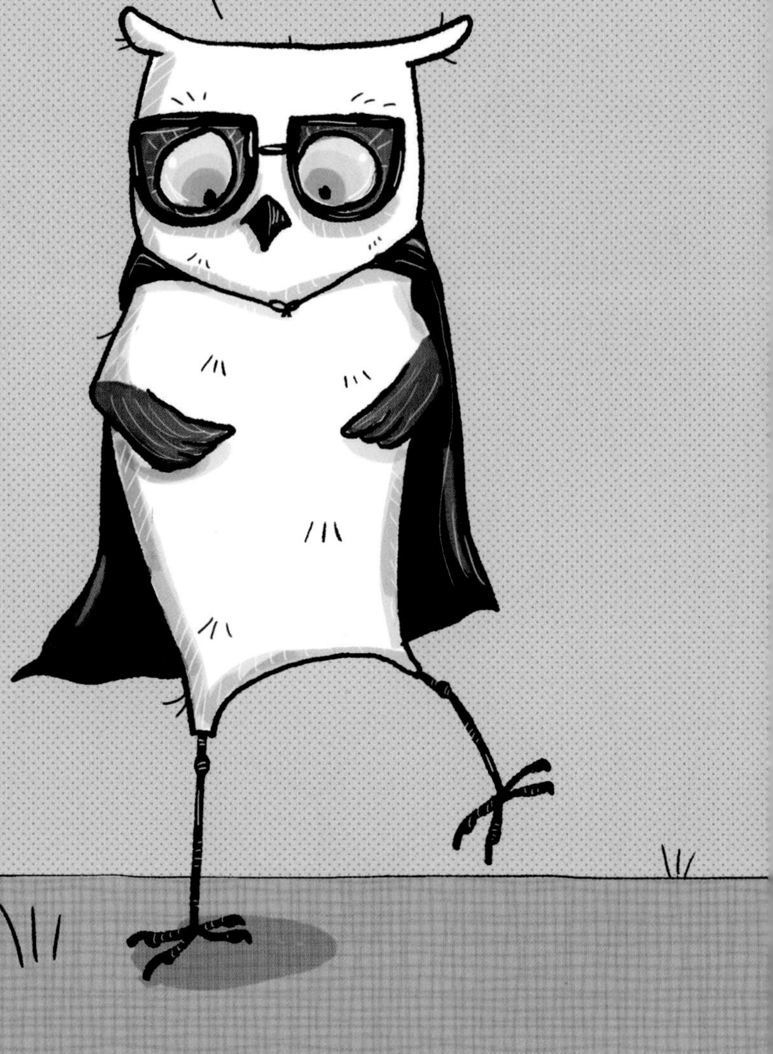

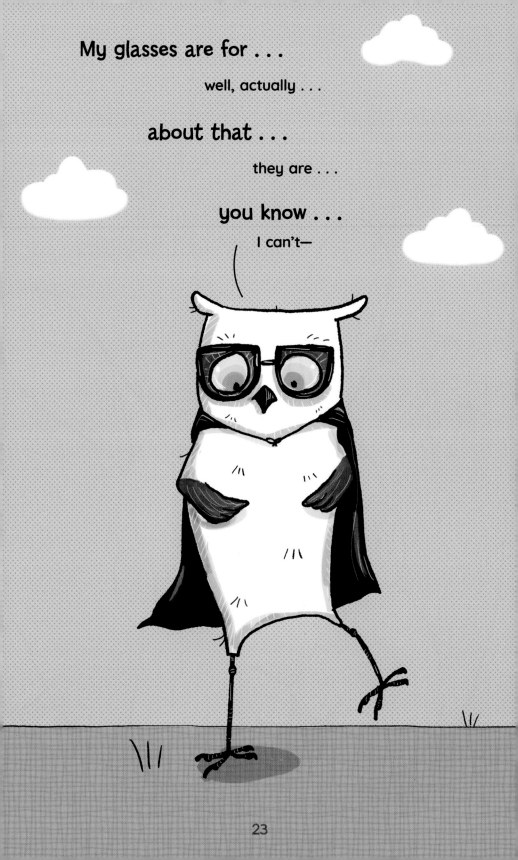

CHAPTER 3
HARE-RAISING

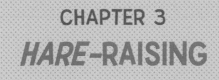

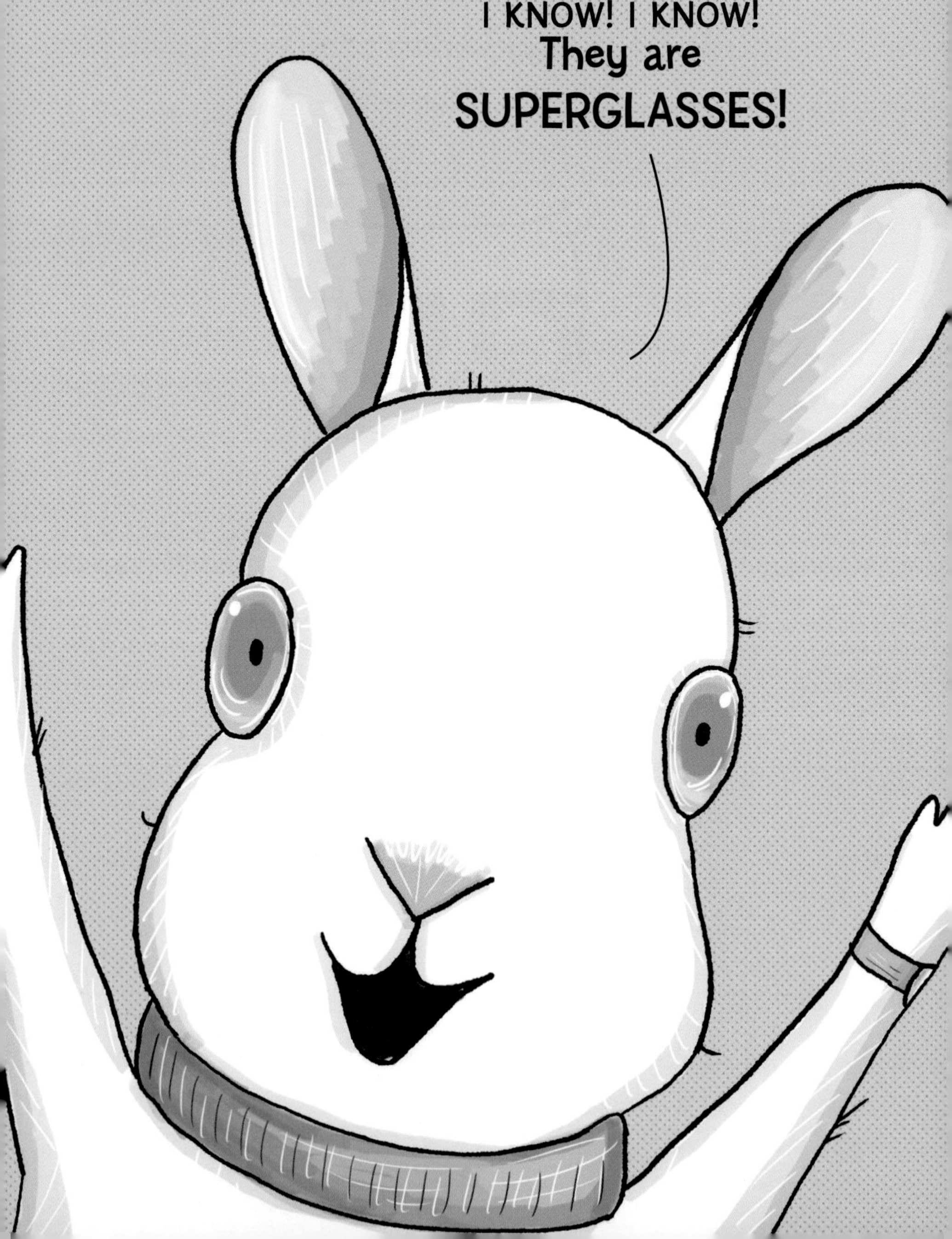
I KNOW! I KNOW! They are SUPERGLASSES!

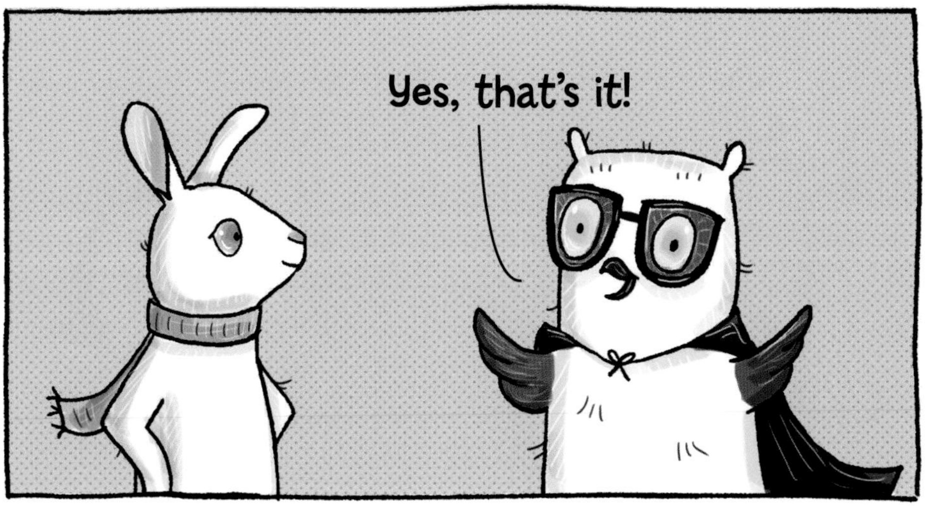
Yes, that's it!

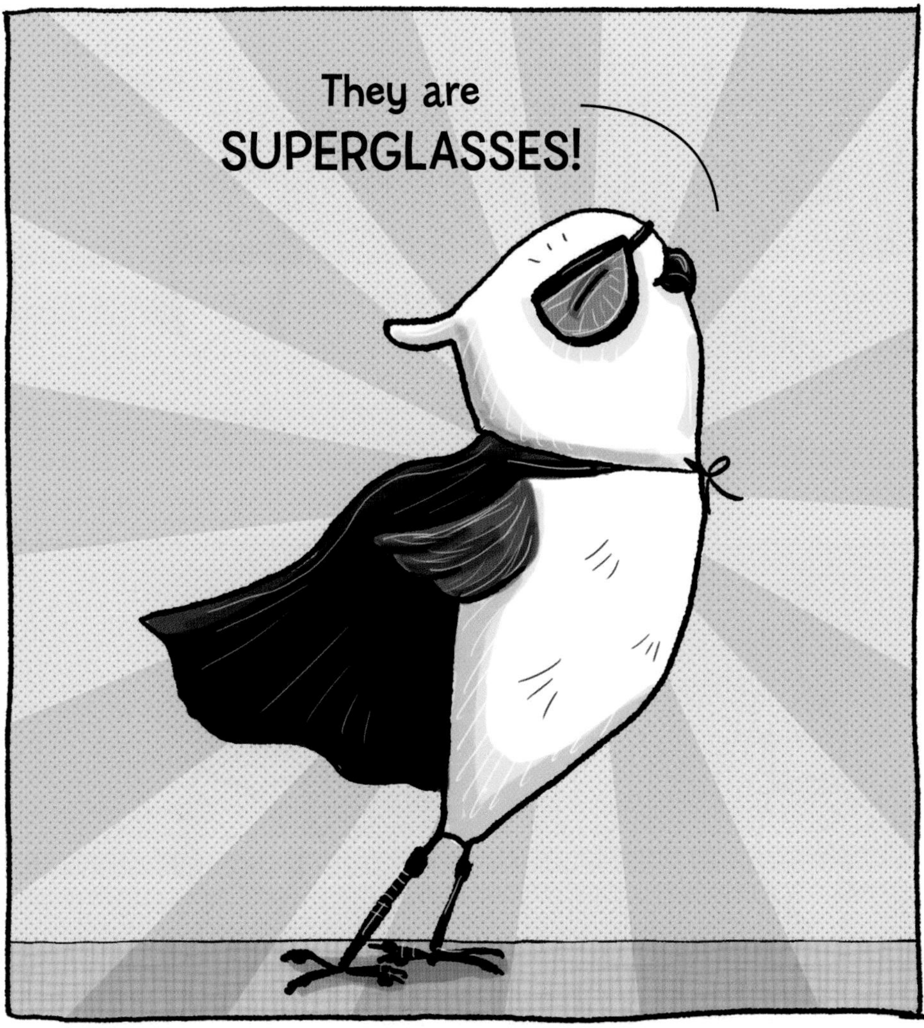
They are
SUPERGLASSES!

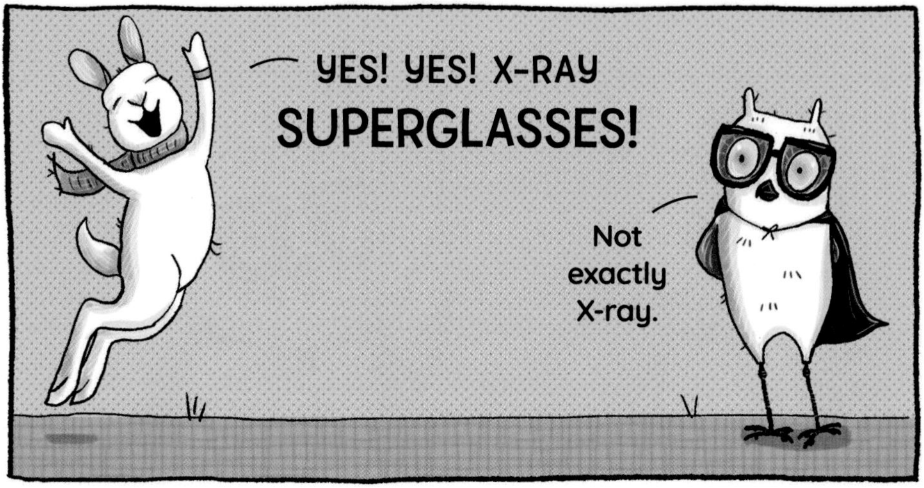
YES! YES! X-RAY SUPERGLASSES!
Not exactly X-ray.

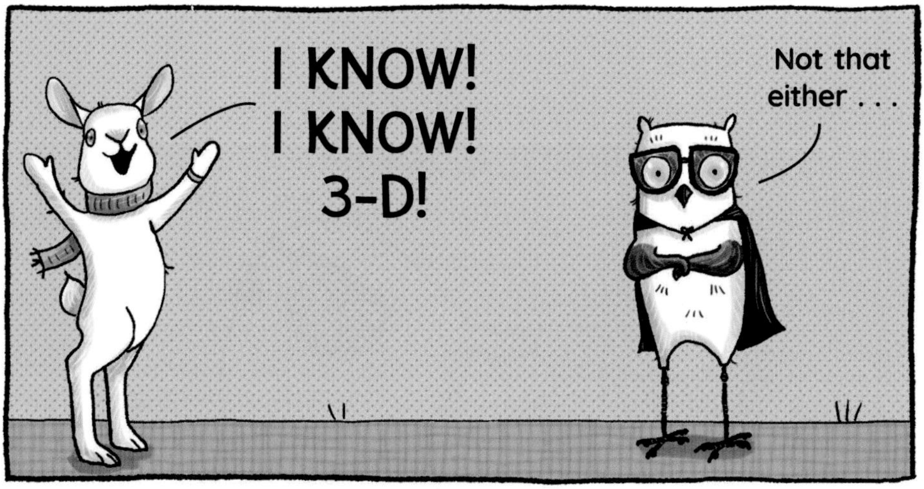
I KNOW! I KNOW! 3-D!
Not that either . . .

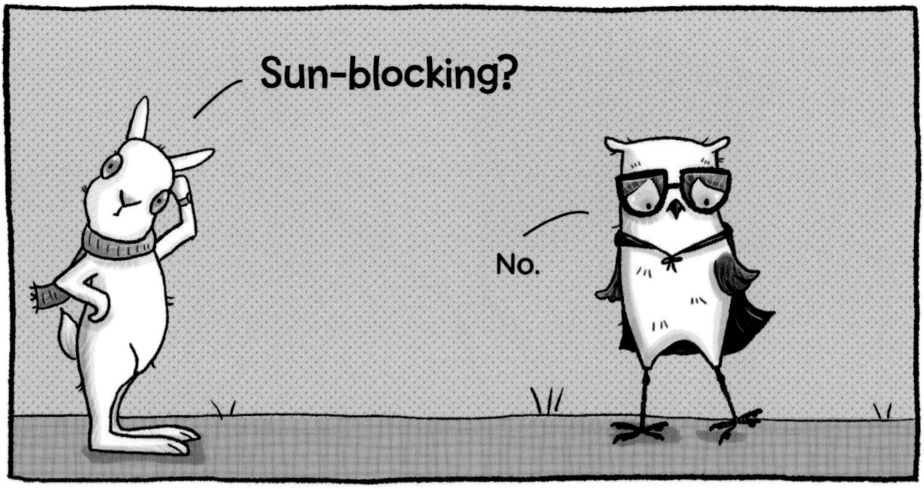
Sun-blocking?
No.

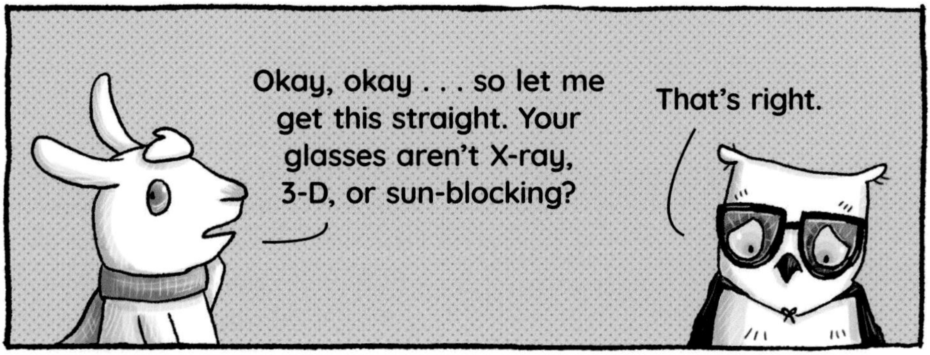
Okay, okay . . . so let me get this straight. Your glasses aren't X-ray, 3-D, or sun-blocking?
That's right.

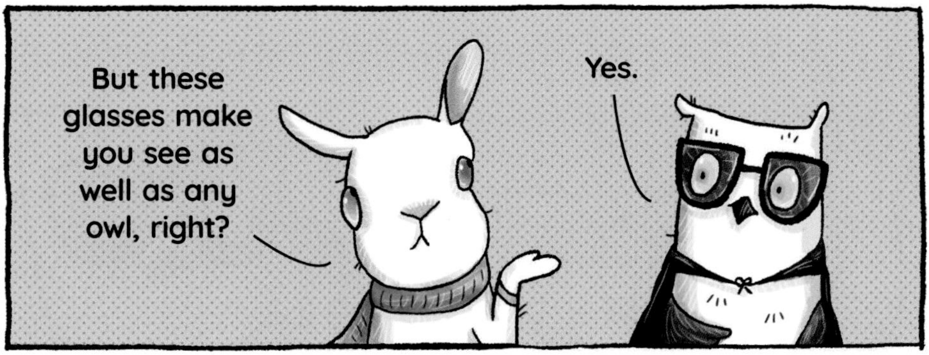
But these glasses make you see as well as any owl, right?
Yes.

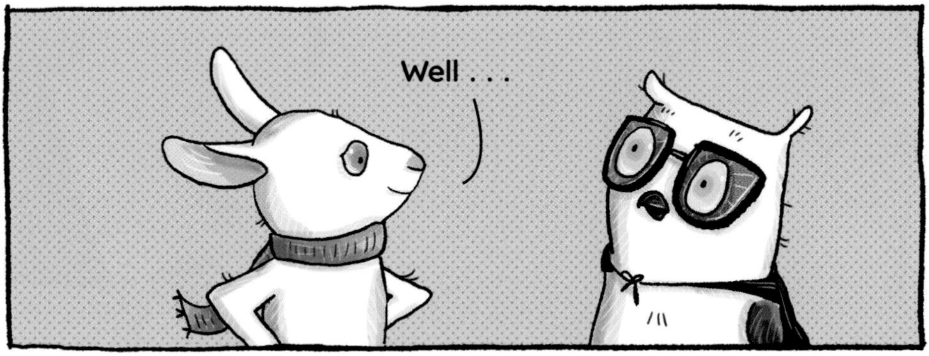
Well . . .

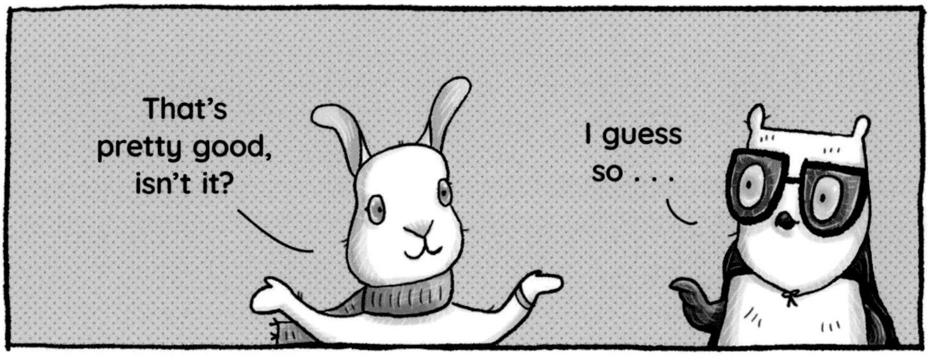
That's pretty good, isn't it?
I guess so . . .

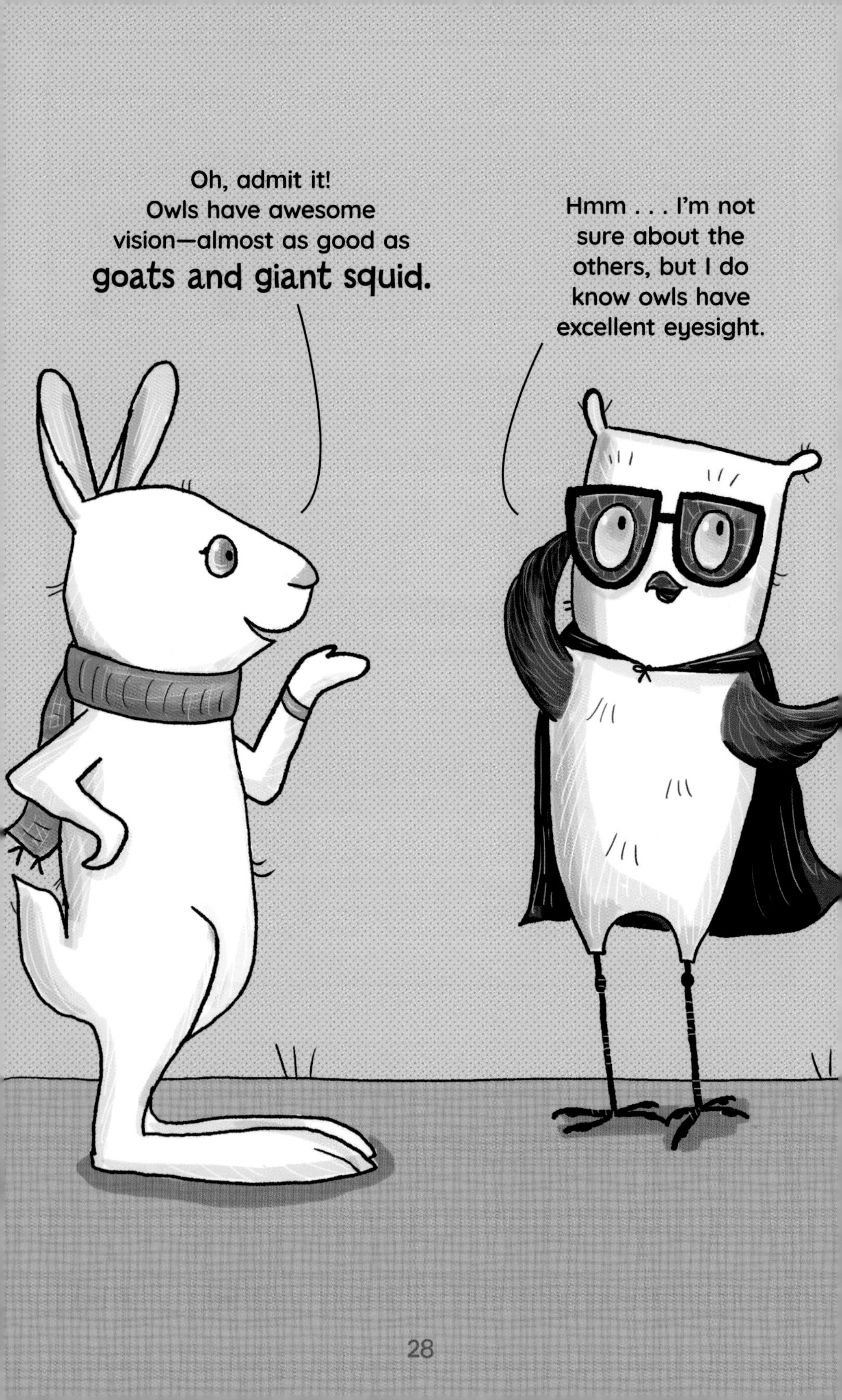
Oh, admit it!
Owls have awesome
vision—almost as good as
goats and giant squid.
Hmm . . . I'm not
sure about the
others, but I do
know owls have
excellent eyesight.

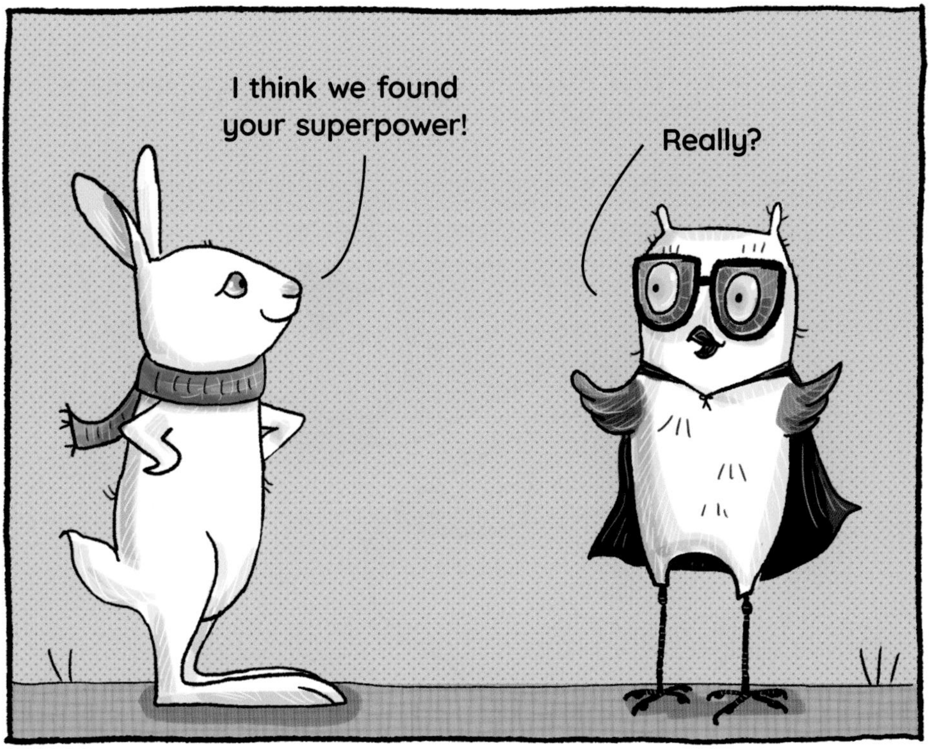
I think we found your superpower!
Really?

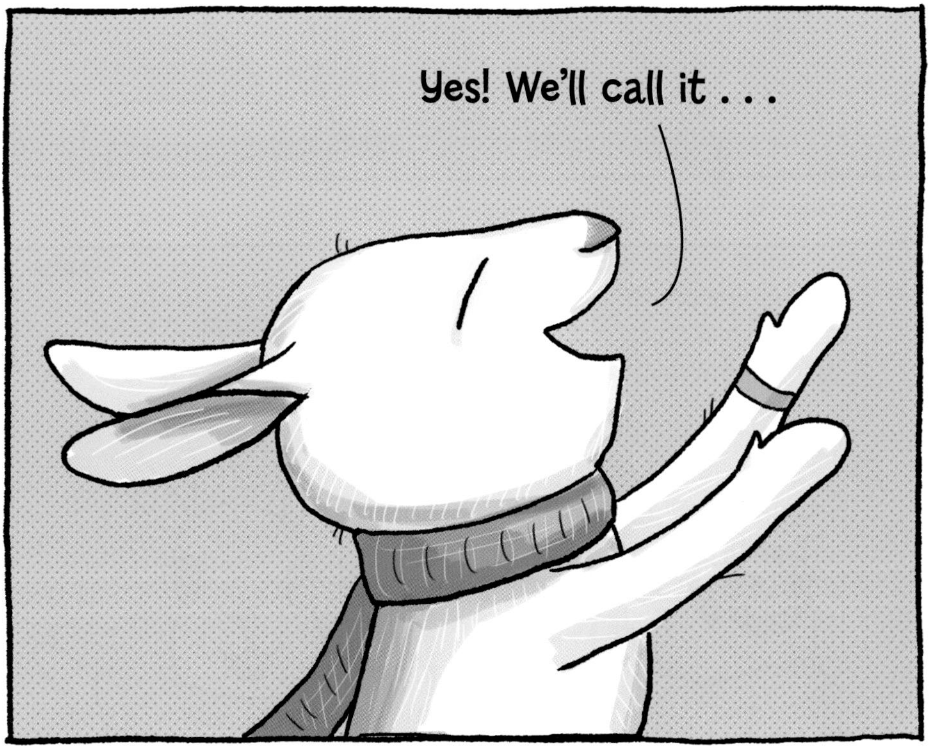
Yes! We'll call it . . .

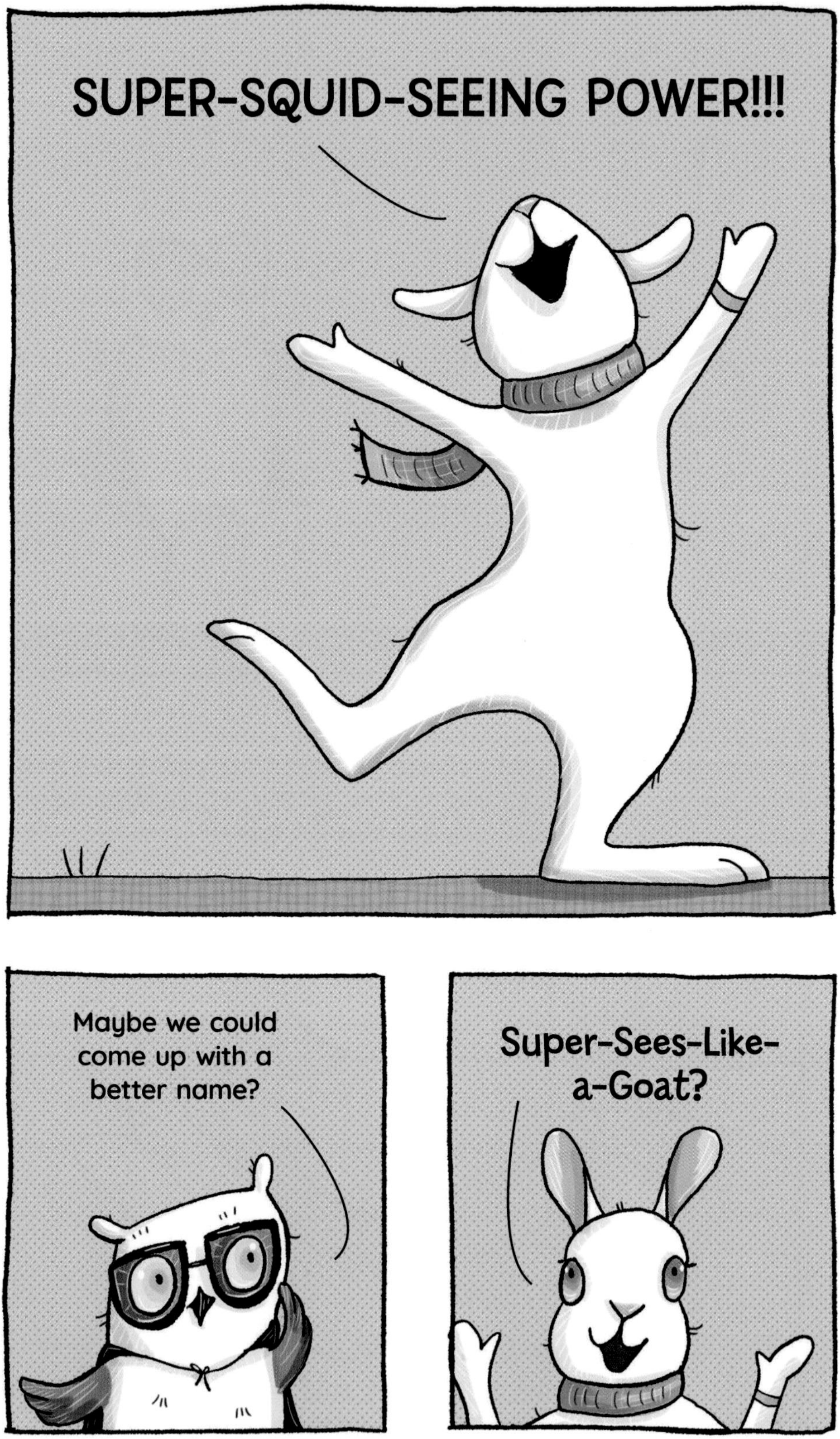
SUPER-SQUID-SEEING POWER!!!
Maybe we could come up with a better name?
Super-Sees-Like-a-Goat?

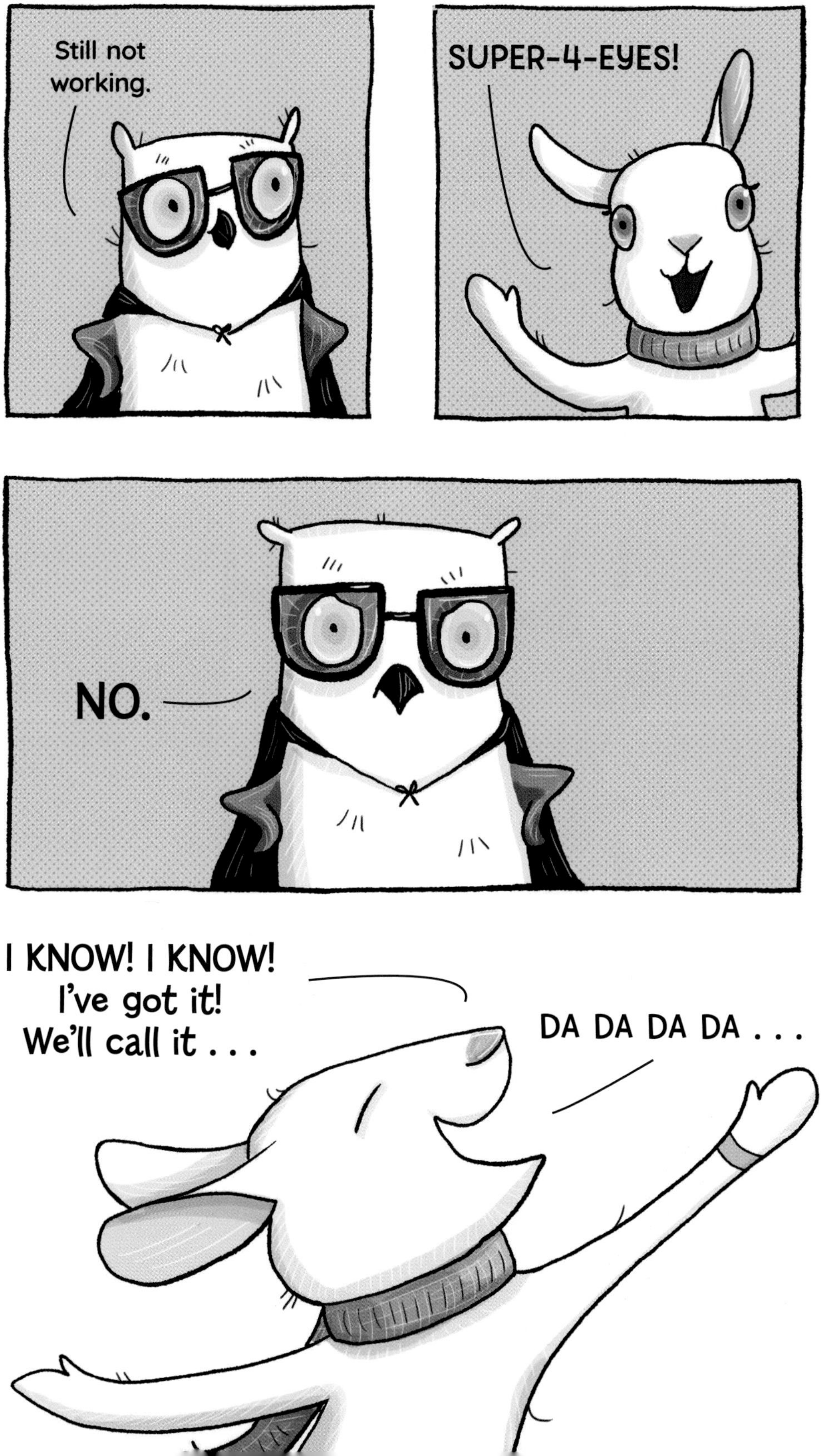
Still not working.
SUPER-4-EYES!
NO.
I KNOW! I KNOW! I've got it! We'll call it . . .
DA DA DA DA . . .

SUPER-VISION!

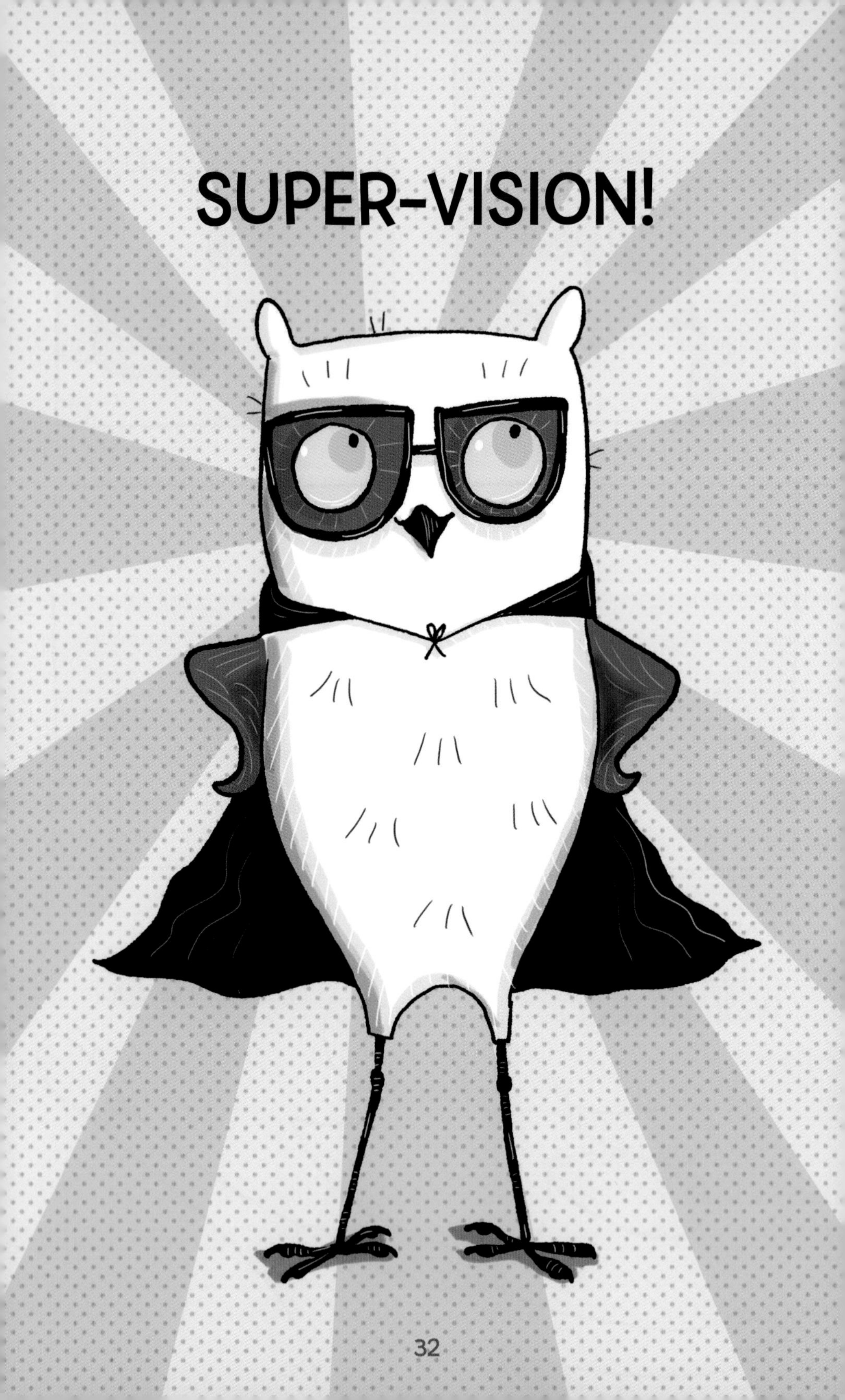

CHAPTER 4
OTTER-LY AWESOME

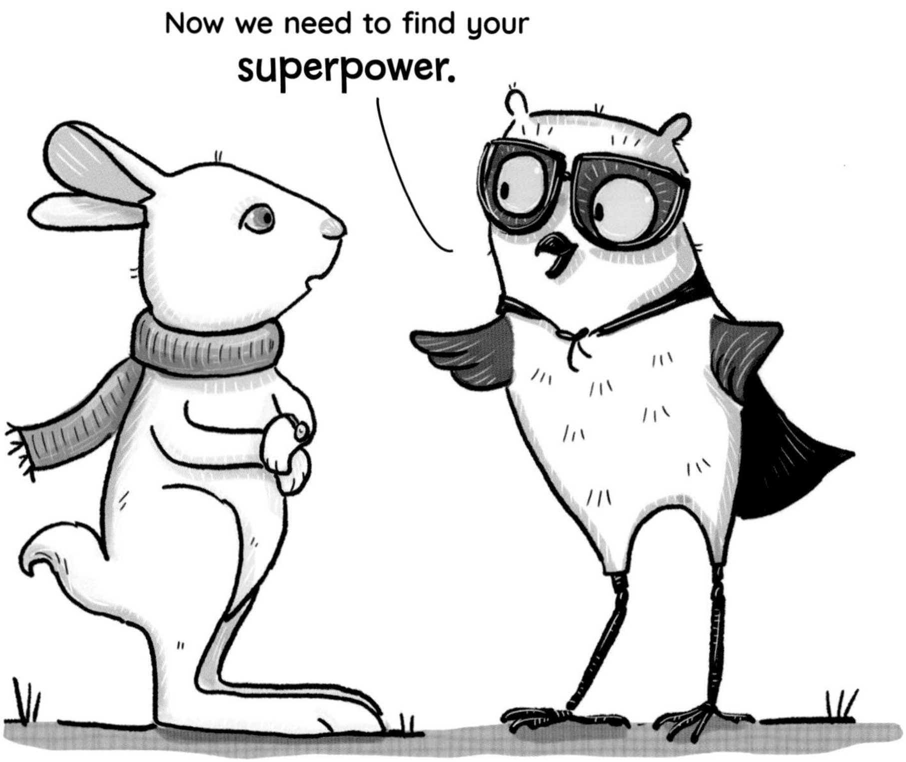
Now we need to find your **superpower.**

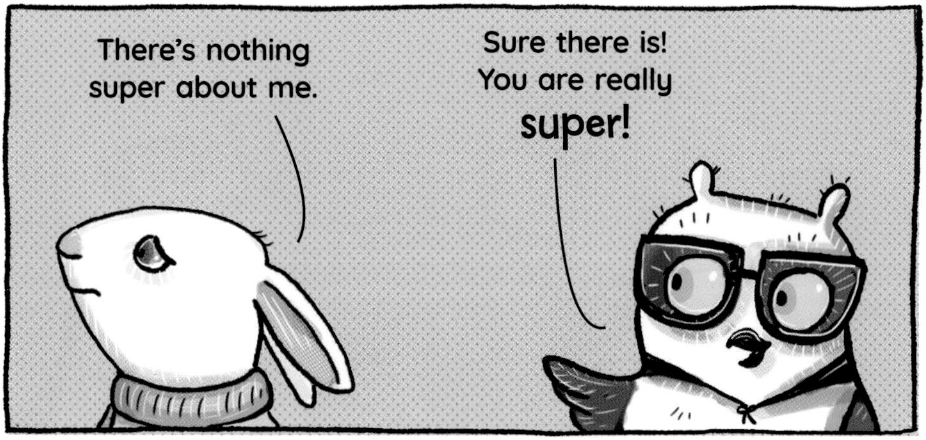
There's nothing super about me.
Sure there is! You are really **super!**

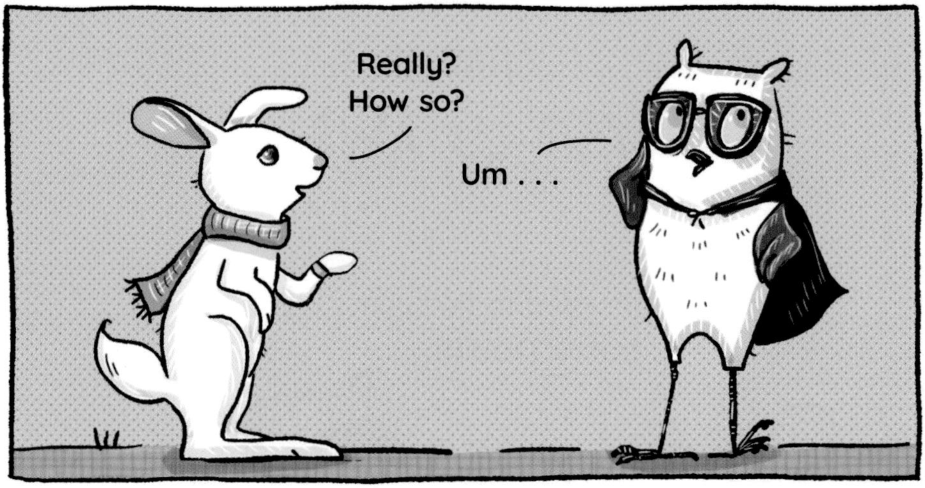
Really?
How so?
Um . . .

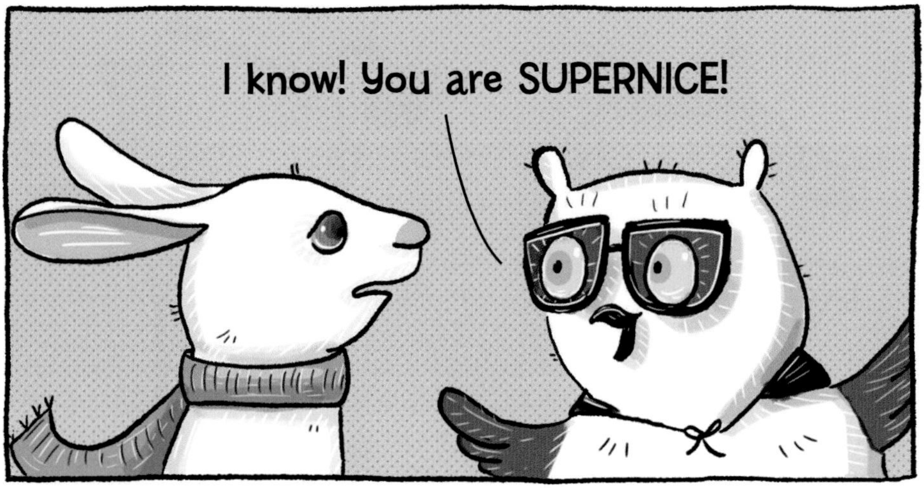
I know! You are SUPERNICE!

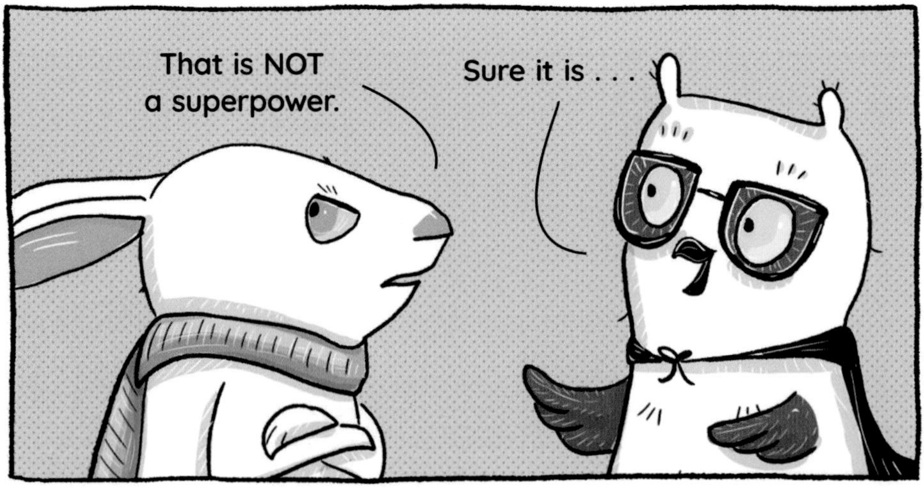
That is NOT
a superpower.
Sure it is . . .

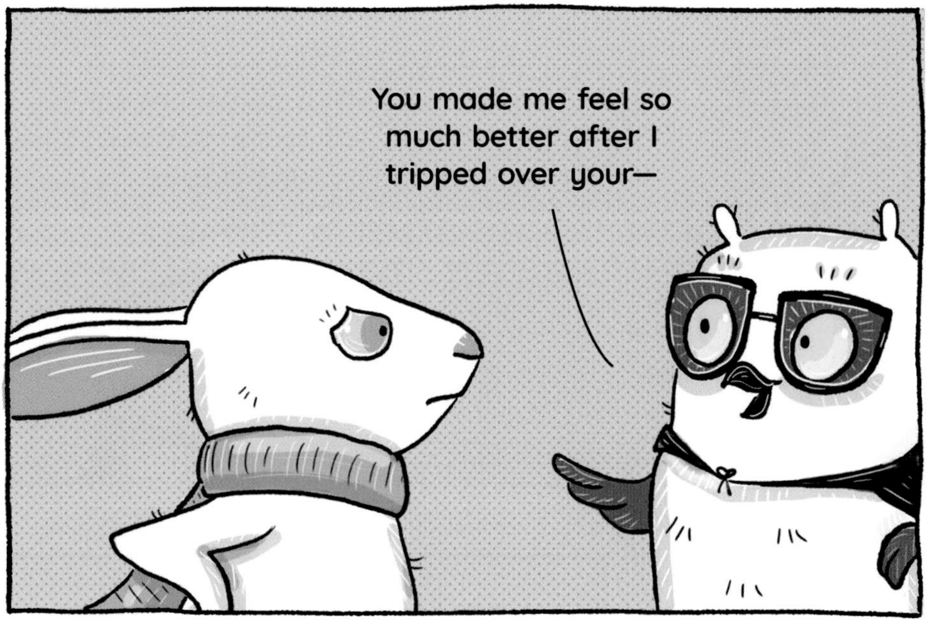
You made me feel so much better after I tripped over your—

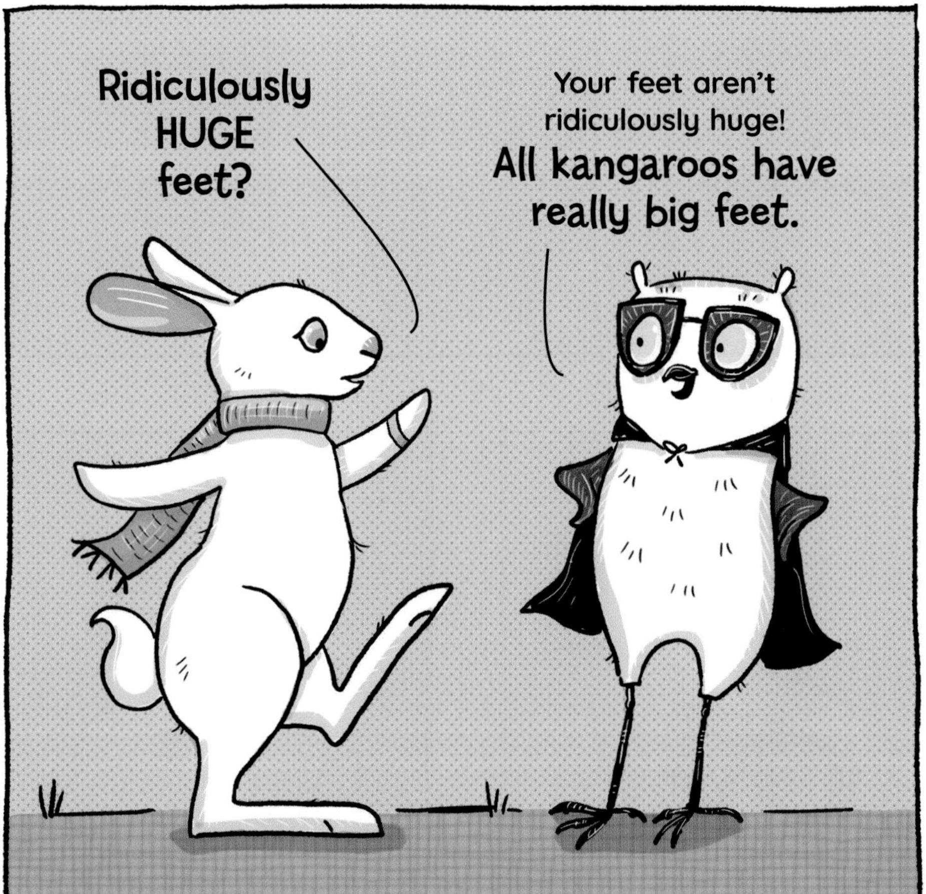
Ridiculously HUGE feet?
Your feet aren't ridiculously huge! All kangaroos have really big feet.

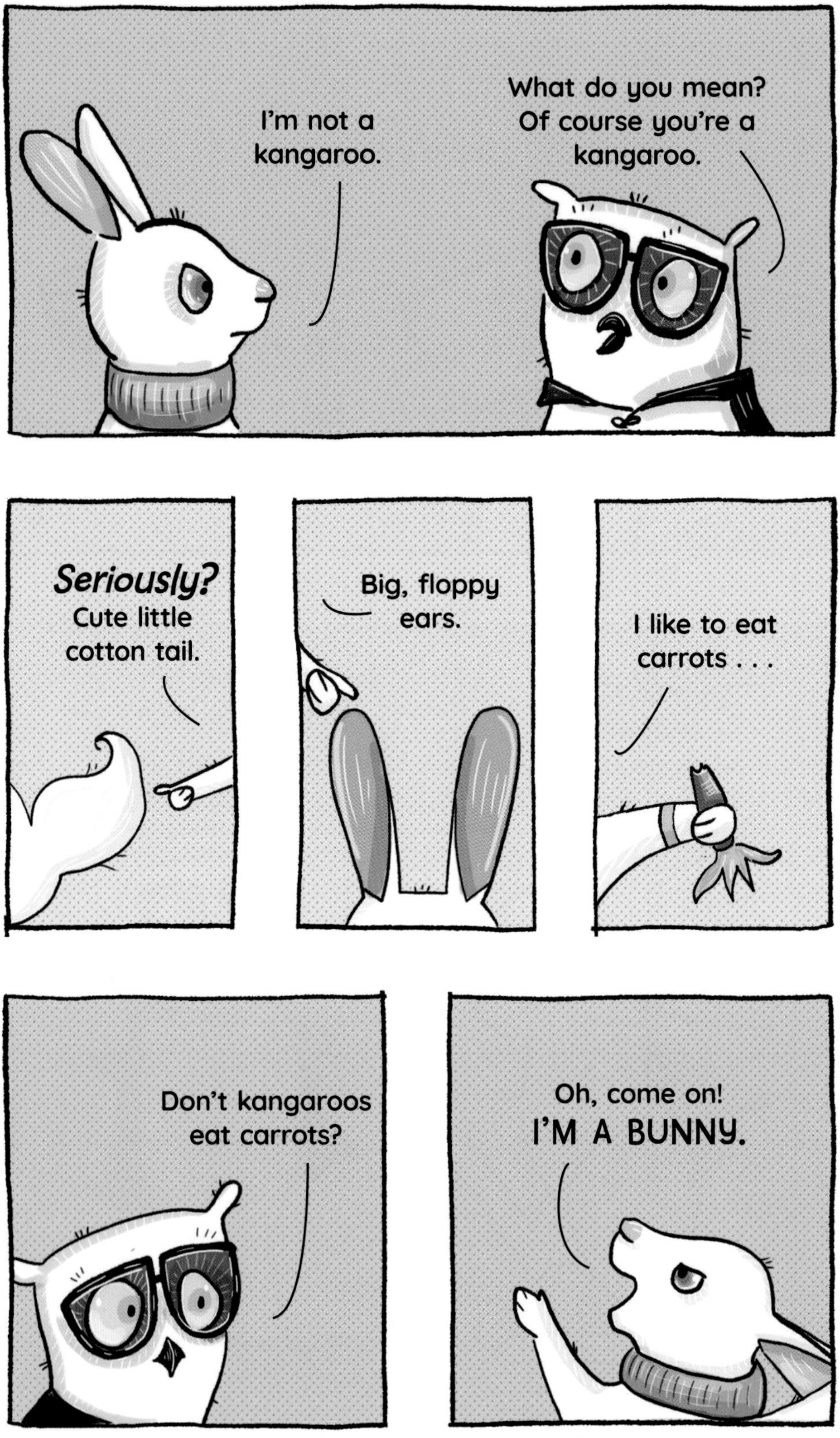
I'm not a kangaroo.
What do you mean? Of course you're a kangaroo.
Seriously? Cute little cotton tail.
Big, floppy ears.
I like to eat carrots . . .
Don't kangaroos eat carrots?
Oh, come on!
I'M A BUNNY.

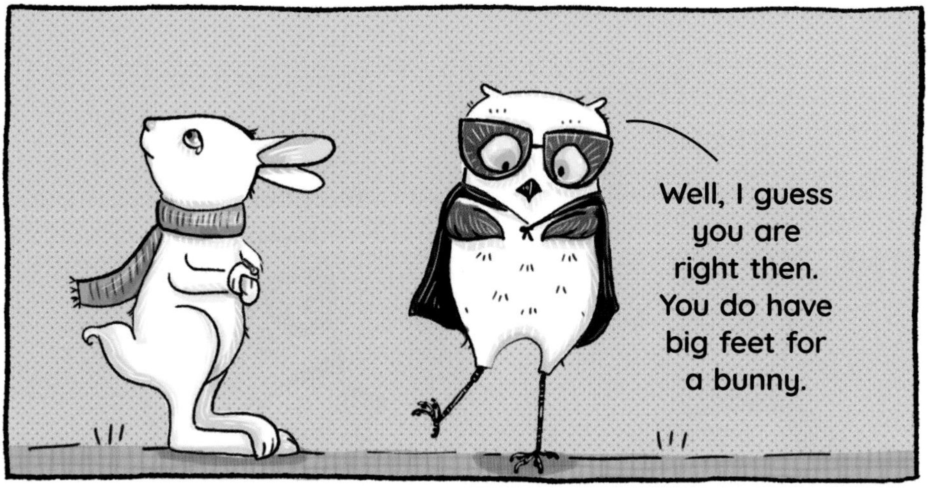
Well, I guess you are right then. You do have big feet for a bunny.

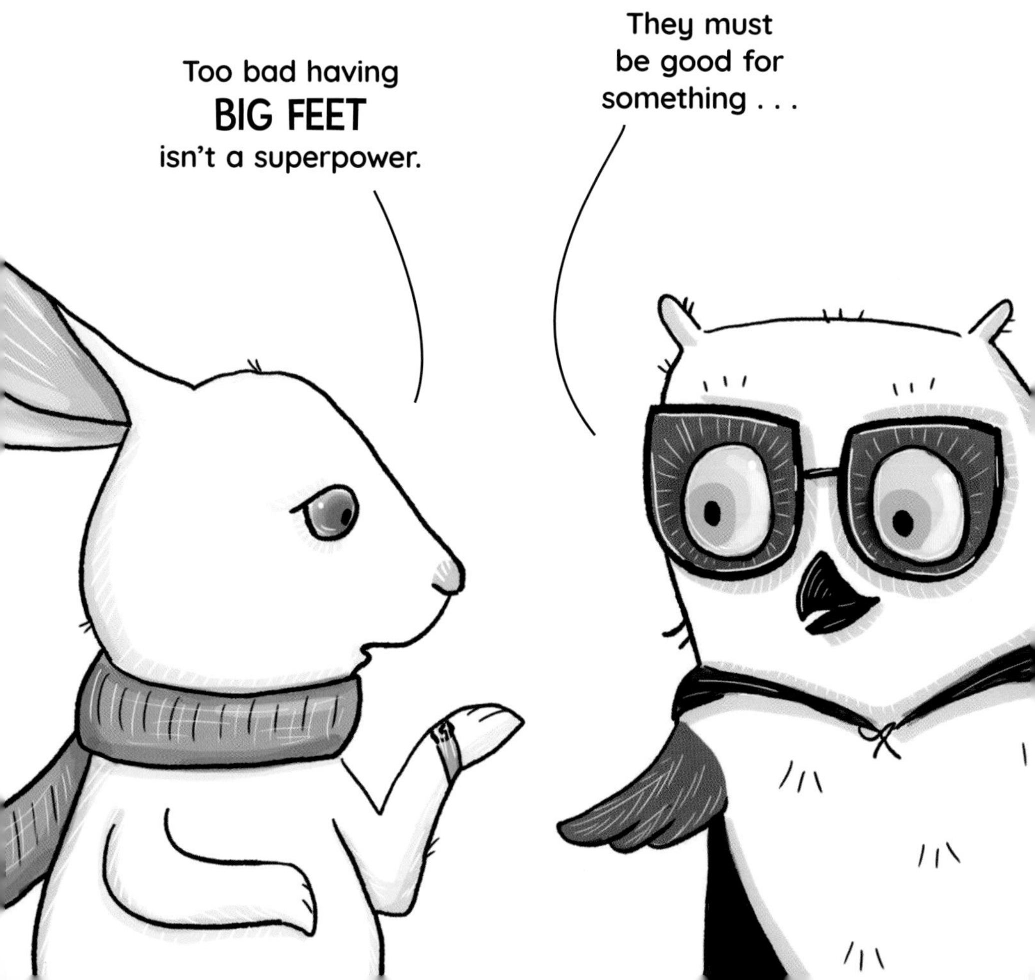
Too bad having BIG FEET isn't a superpower.
They must be good for something . . .

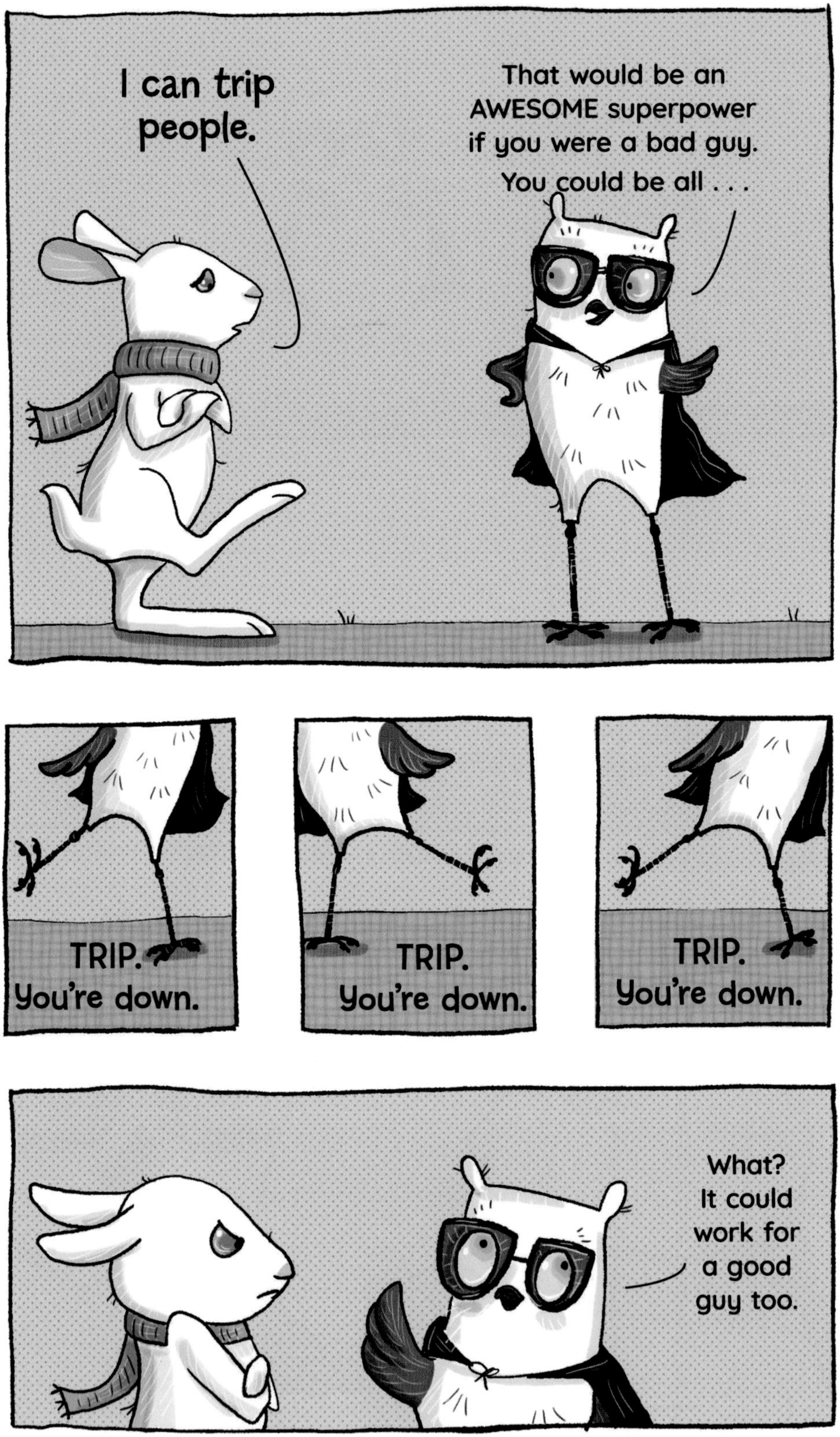
I can trip people.
That would be an AWESOME superpower if you were a bad guy. You could be all . . .
TRIP. You're down.
TRIP. You're down.
TRIP. You're down.
What? It could work for a good guy too.

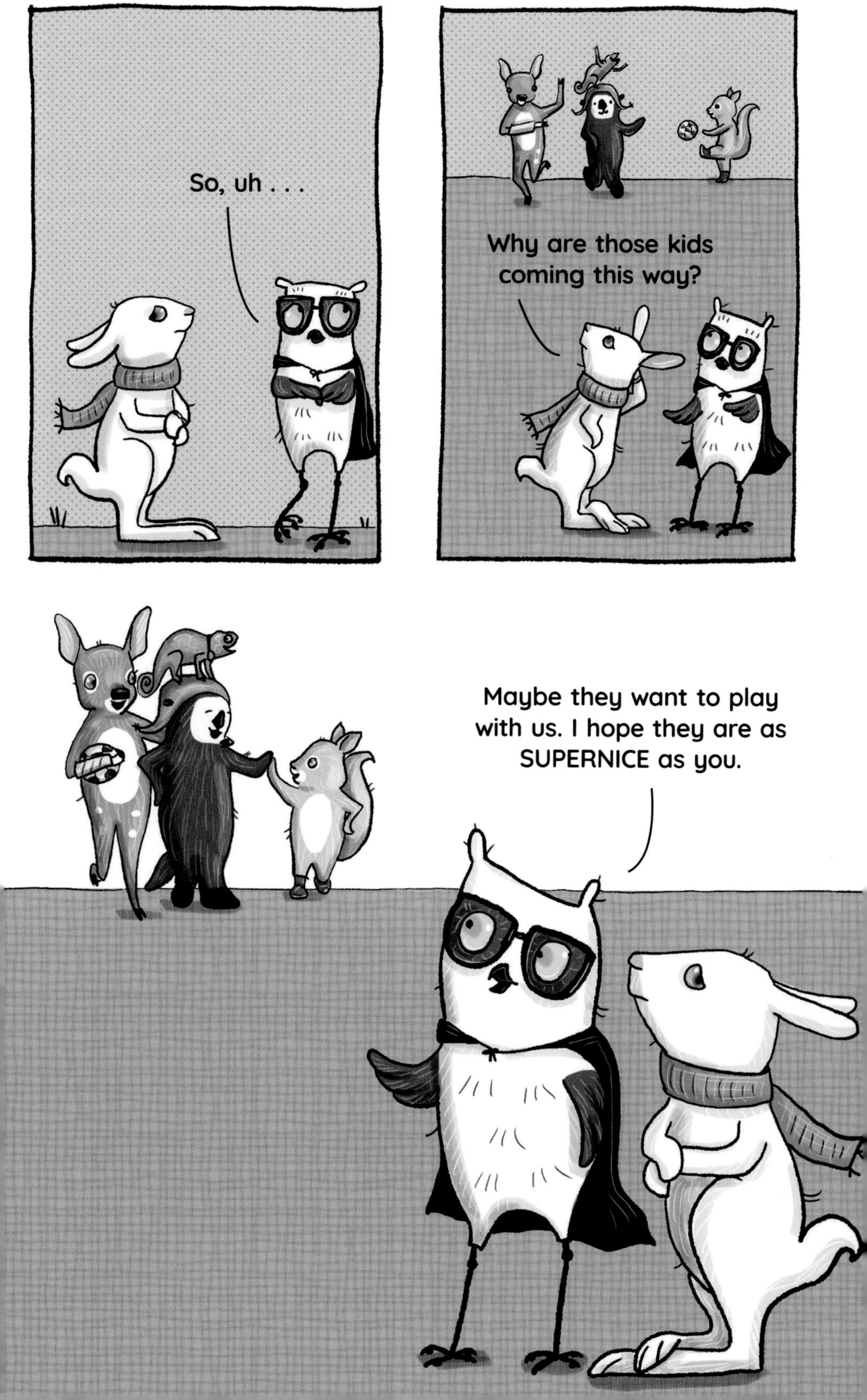
So, uh . . .
Why are those kids coming this way?
Maybe they want to play with us. I hope they are as SUPERNICE as you.

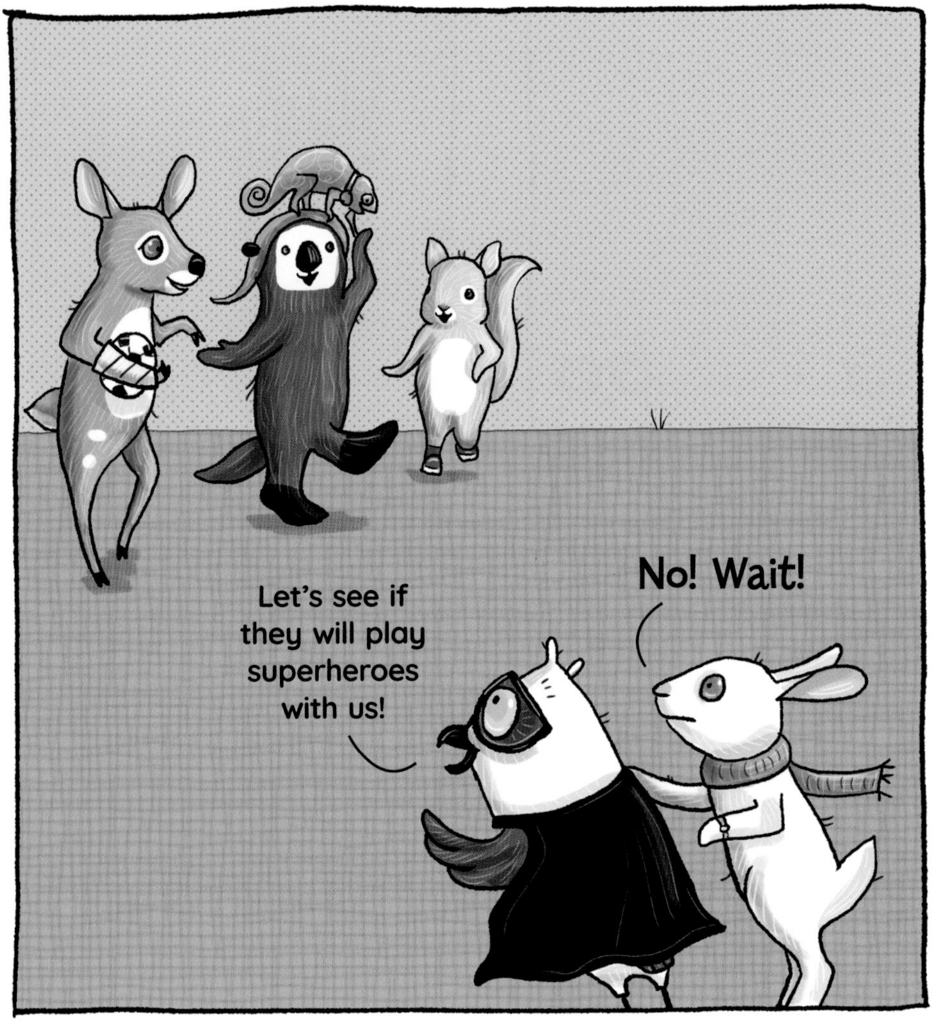
Let's see if they will play superheroes with us!
No! Wait!

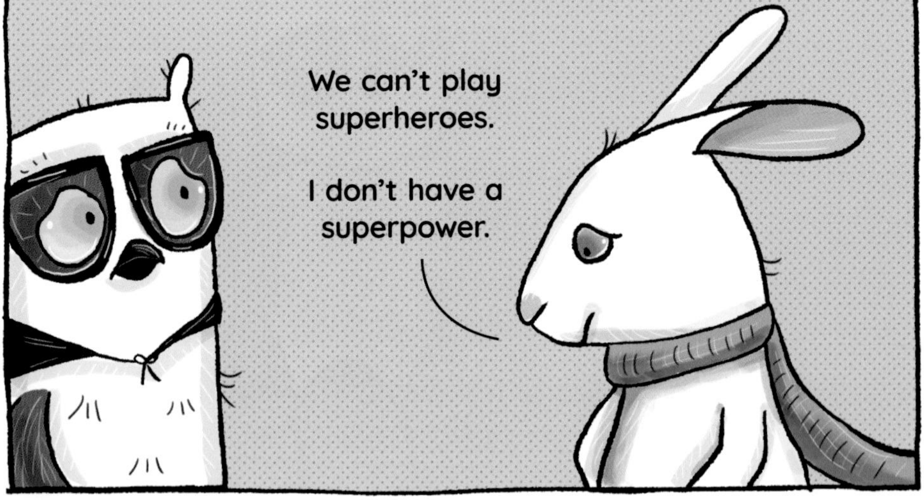
We can't play superheroes.
I don't have a superpower.

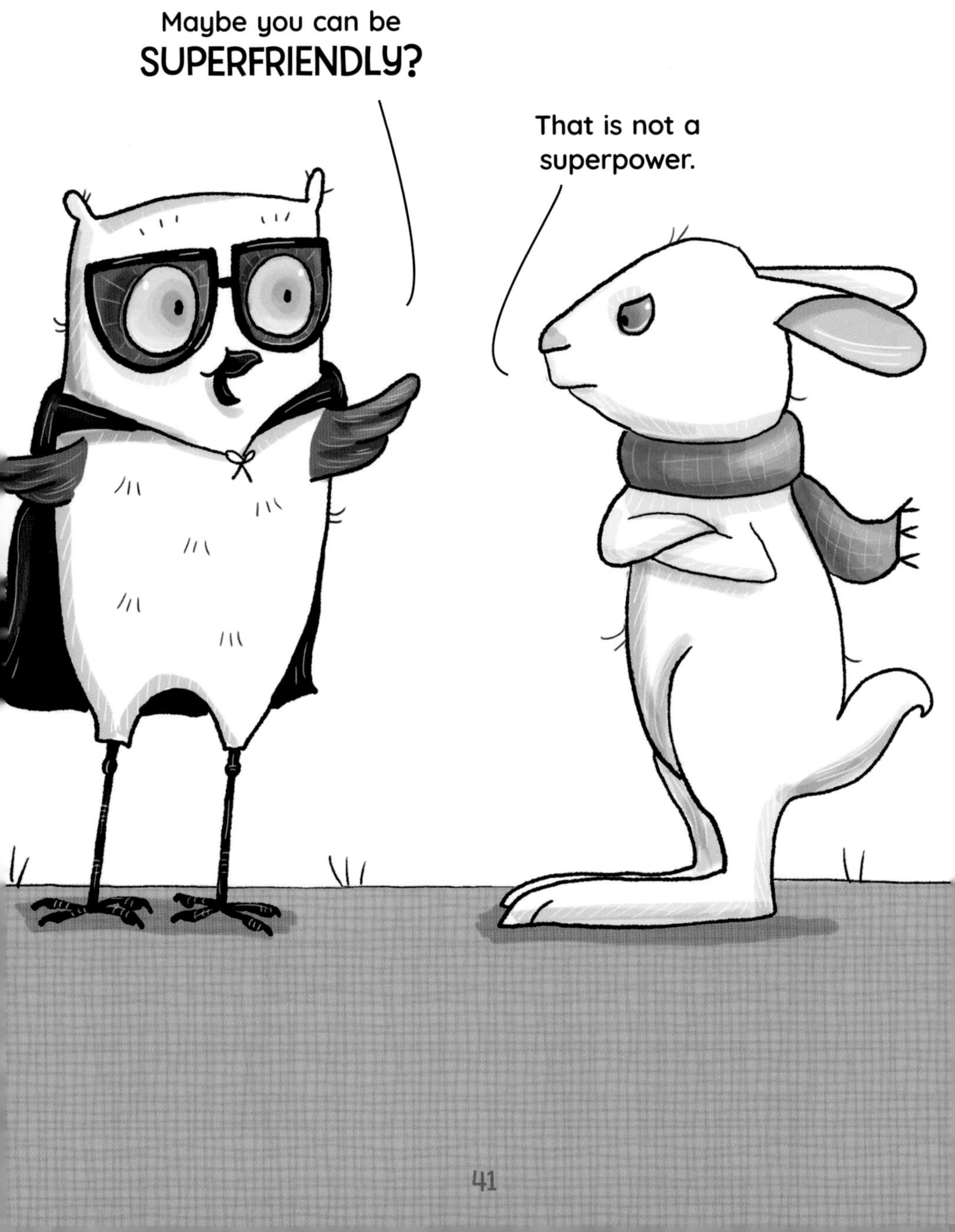
Maybe you can be **SUPERFRIENDLY?**
That is not a superpower.

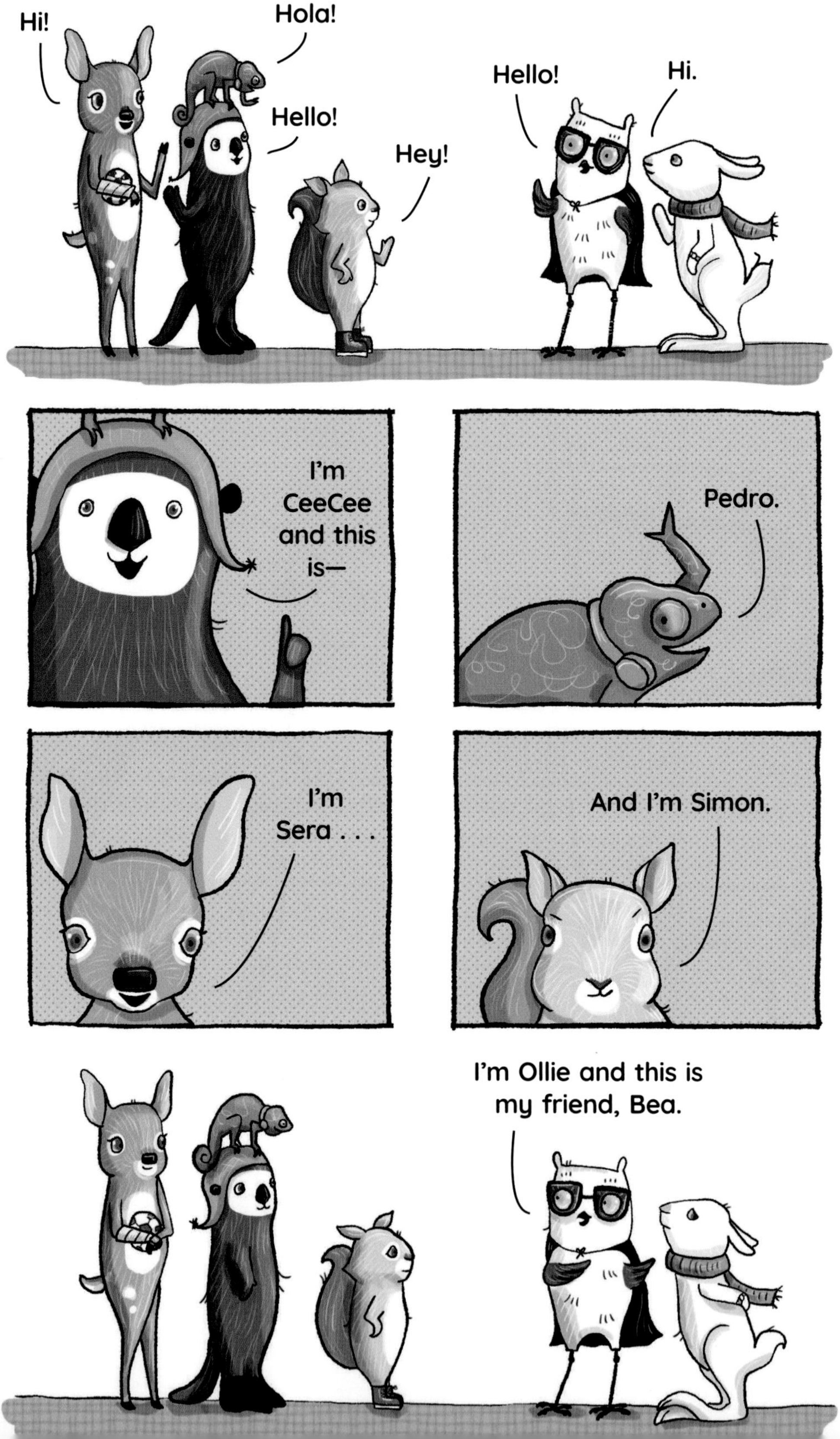
Hi!
Hola!
Hello!
Hey!
Hello!
Hi.
I'm CeeCee and this is—
Pedro.
I'm Sera . . .
And I'm Simon.
I'm Ollie and this is my friend, Bea.

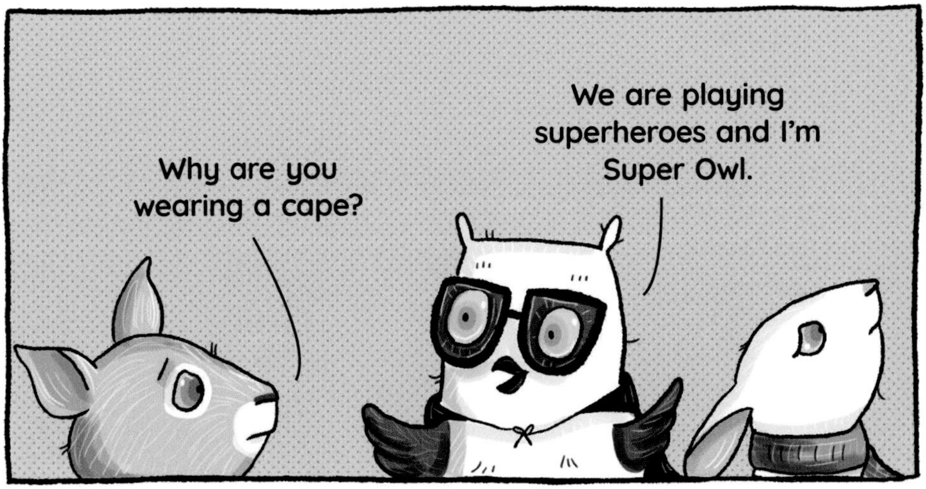
Why are you wearing a cape?
We are playing superheroes and I'm Super Owl.

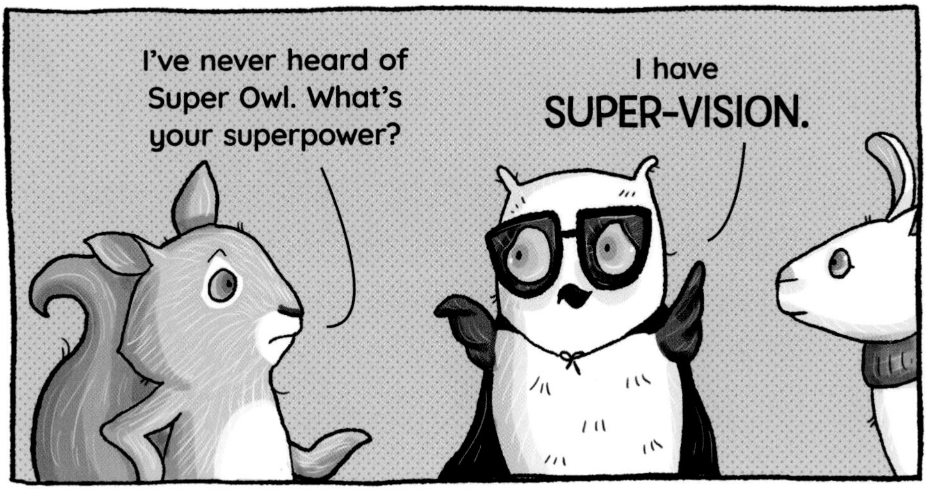
I've never heard of Super Owl. What's your superpower?
I have SUPER-VISION.

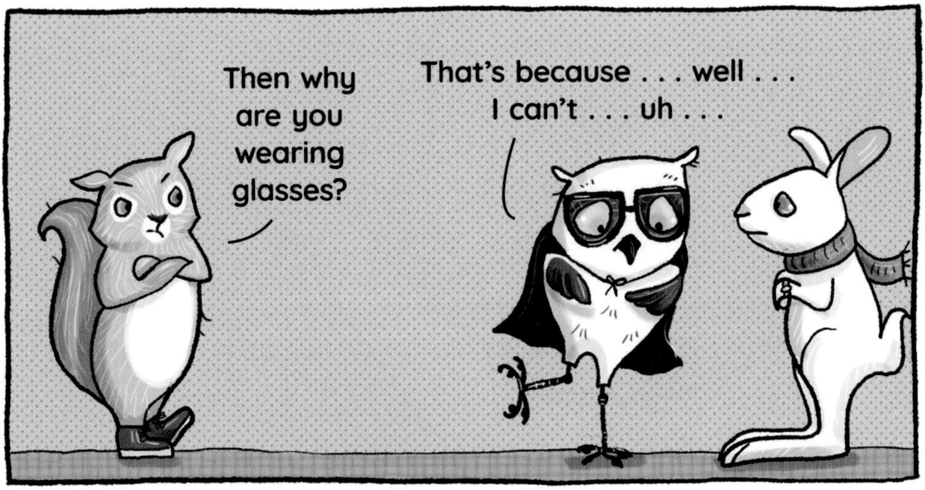
Then why are you wearing glasses?
That's because . . . well . . . I can't . . . uh . . .

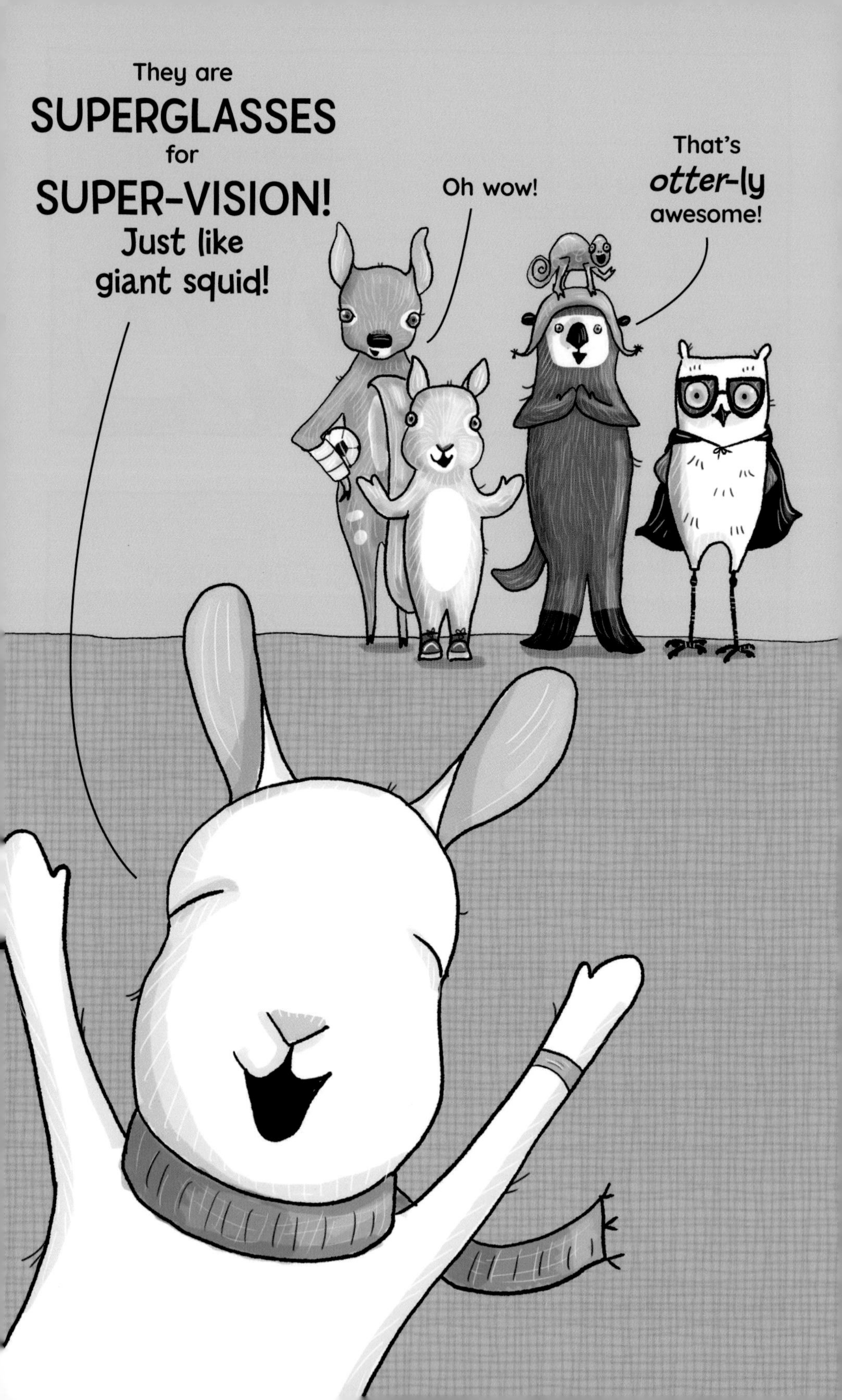

They are SUPERGLASSES for SUPER-VISION! Just like giant squid!
Oh wow!
That's *otter*-ly awesome!

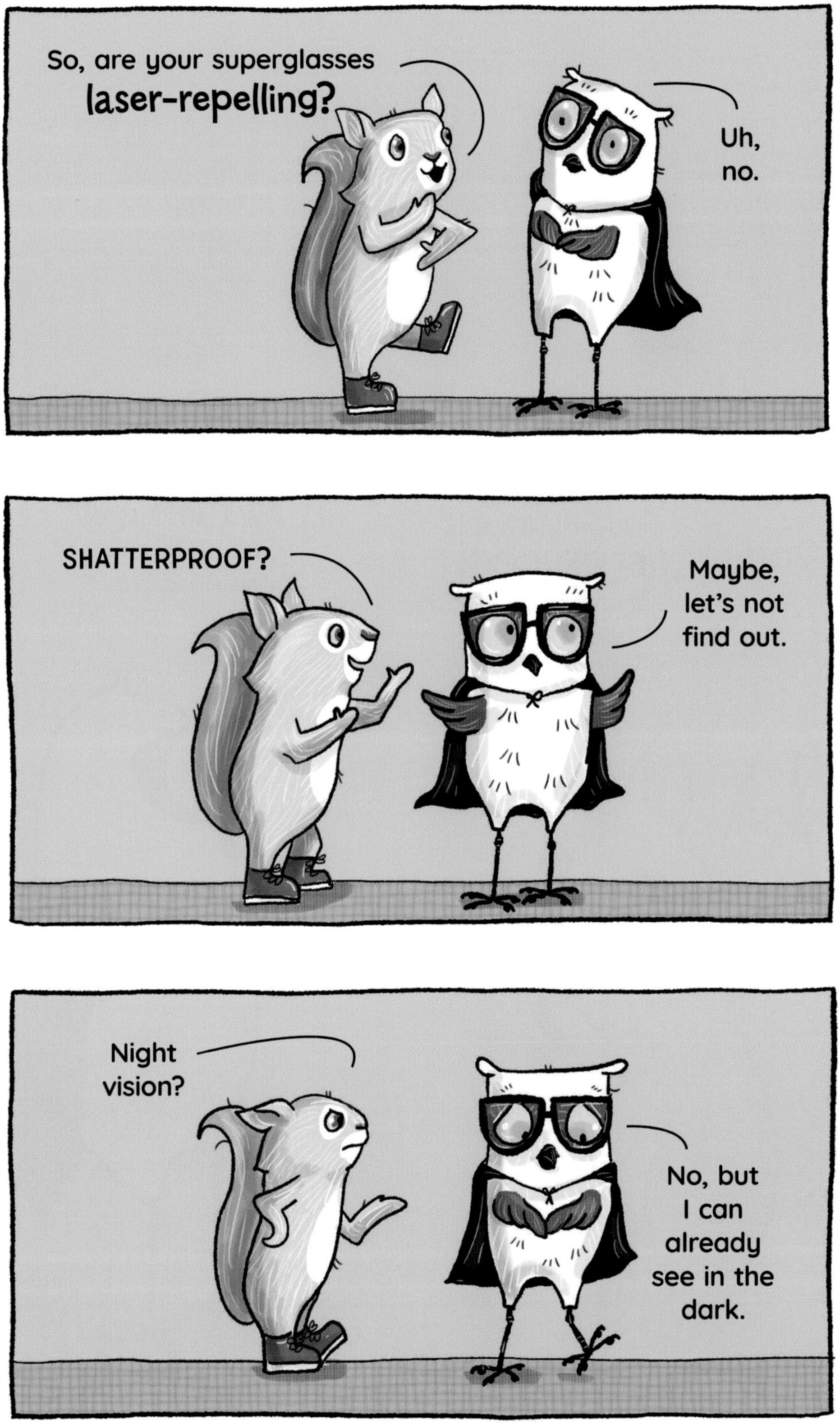
So, are your superglasses laser-repelling?
Uh, no.
SHATTERPROOF?
Maybe, let's not find out.
Night vision?
No, but I can already see in the dark.

CHAPTER 5

SQUIRREL-LOCK HOLMES

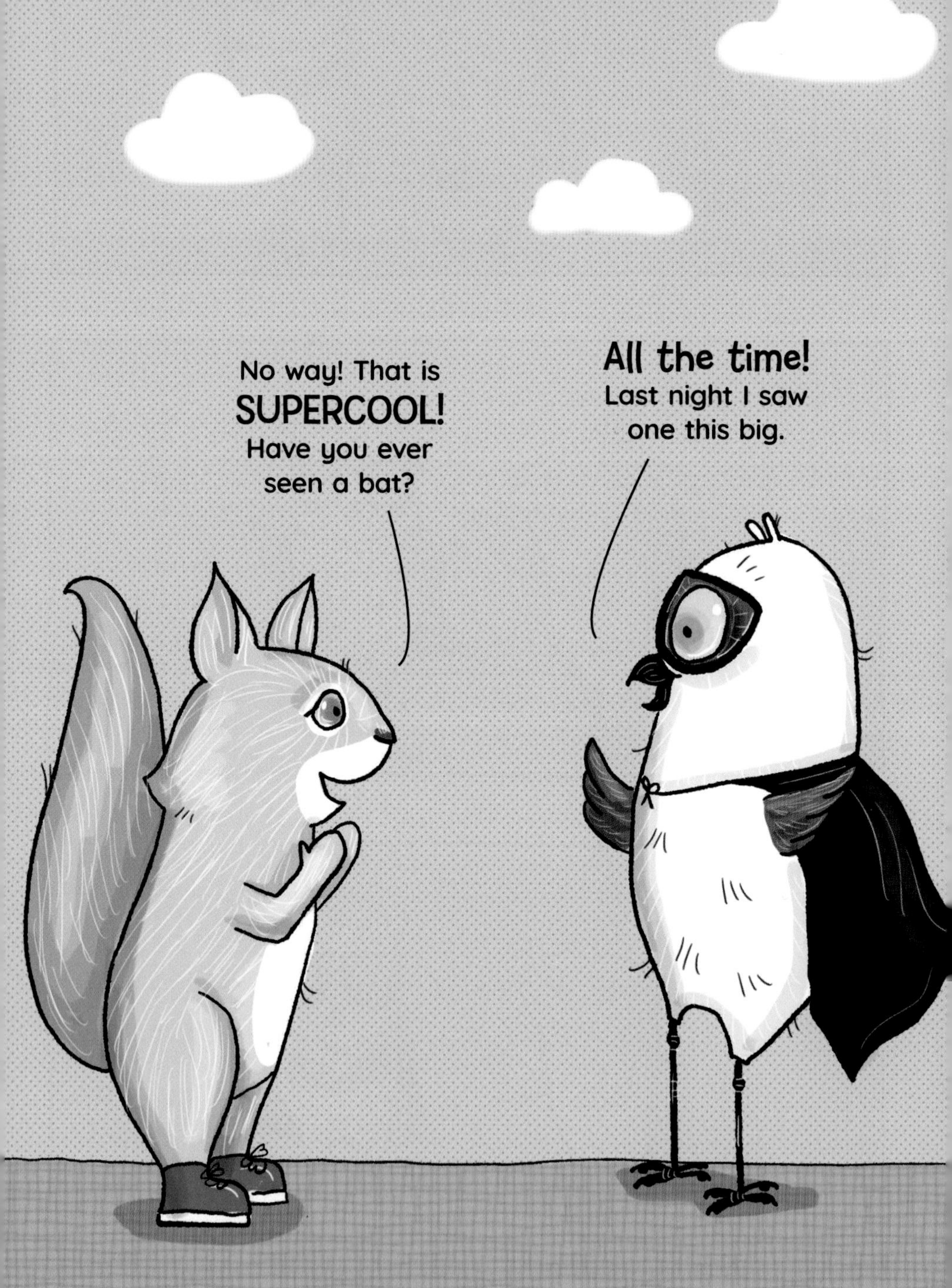
No way! That is SUPERCOOL! Have you ever seen a bat?
All the time! Last night I saw one this big.

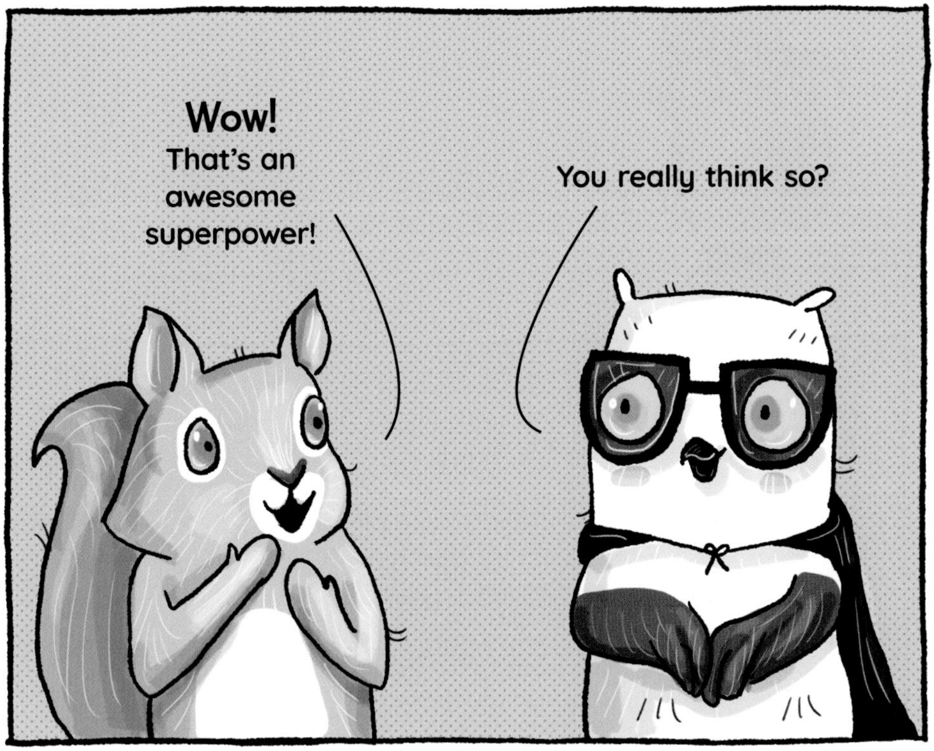
Wow!
That's an
awesome
superpower!
You really think so?

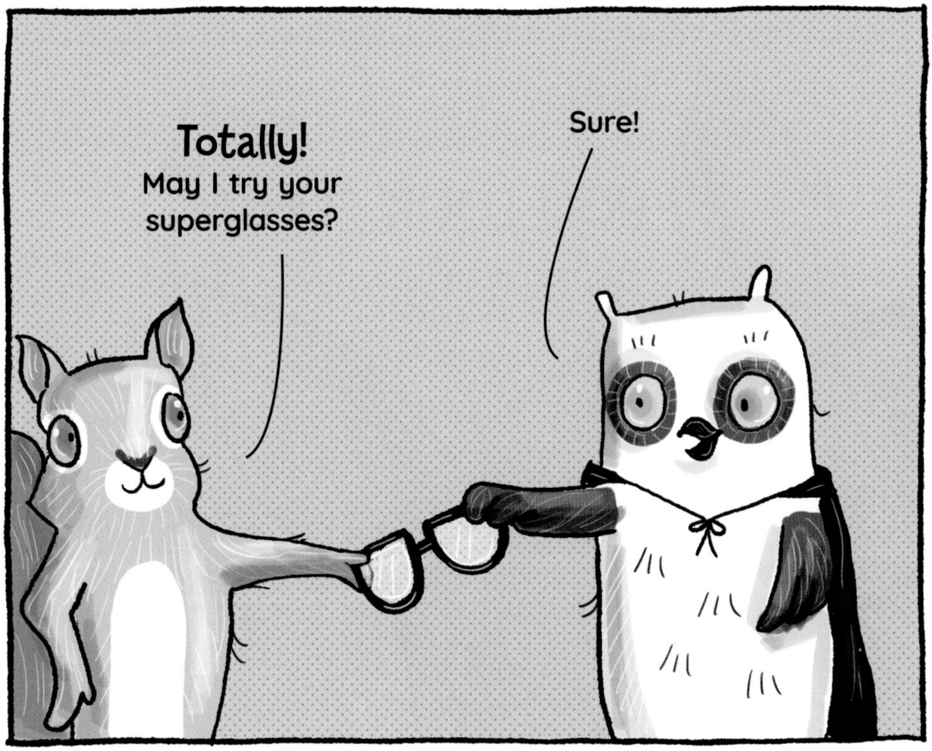
Totally!
May I try your
superglasses?
Sure!

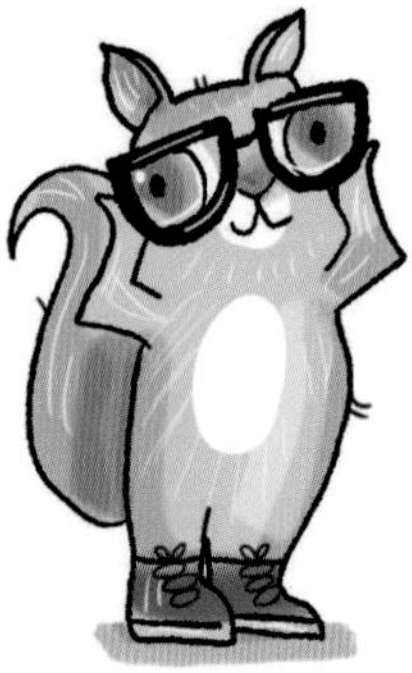

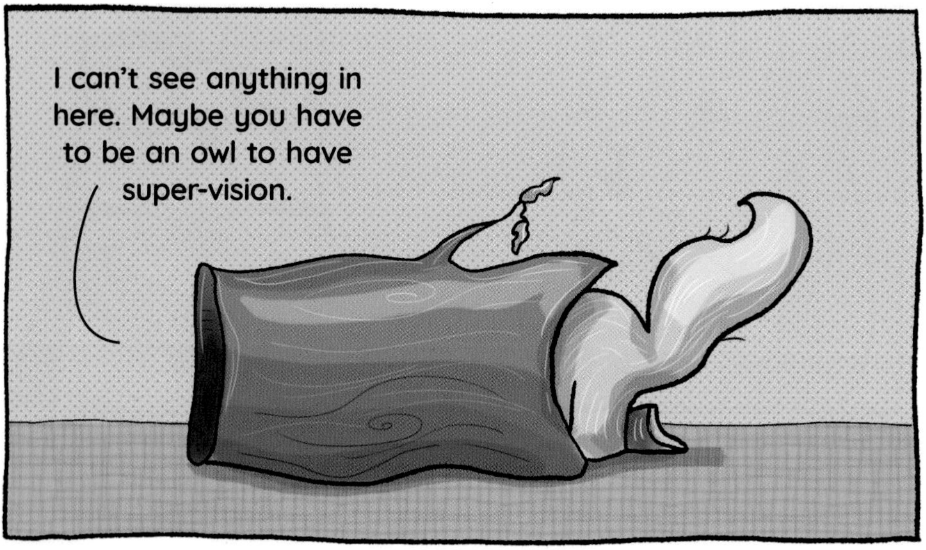
I can't see anything in here. Maybe you have to be an owl to have super-vision.

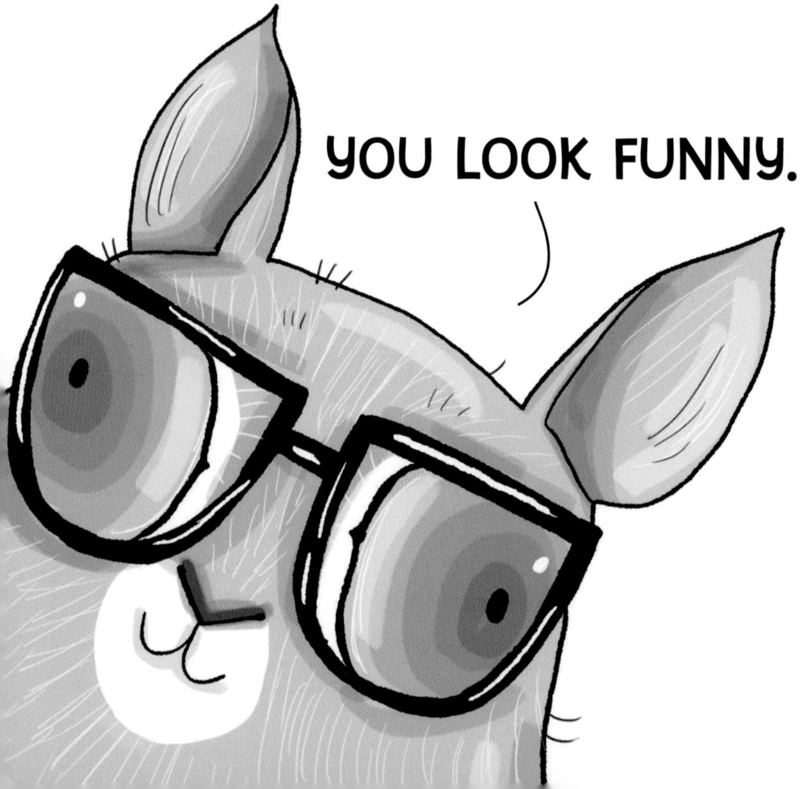
YOU LOOK FUNNY.

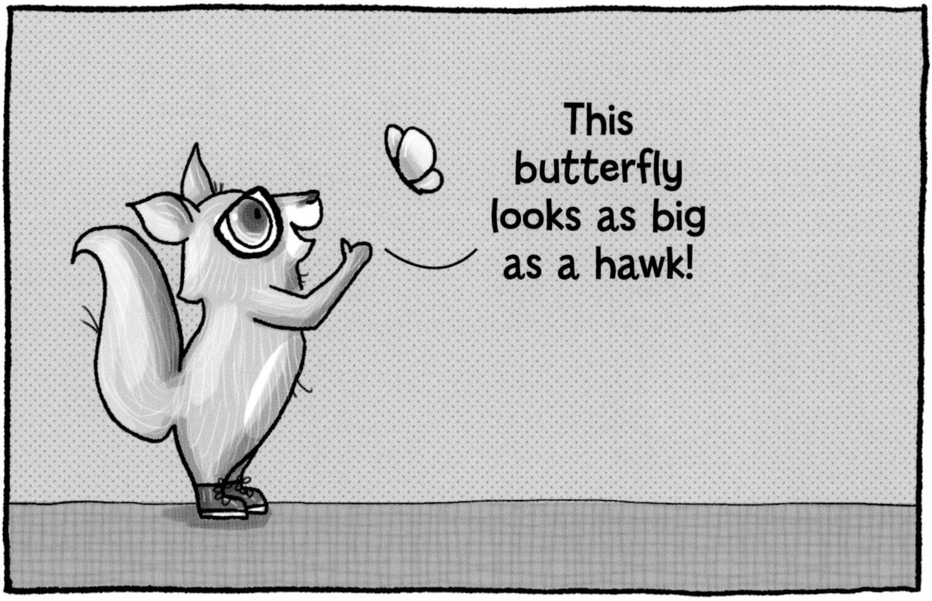
This butterfly looks as big as a hawk!

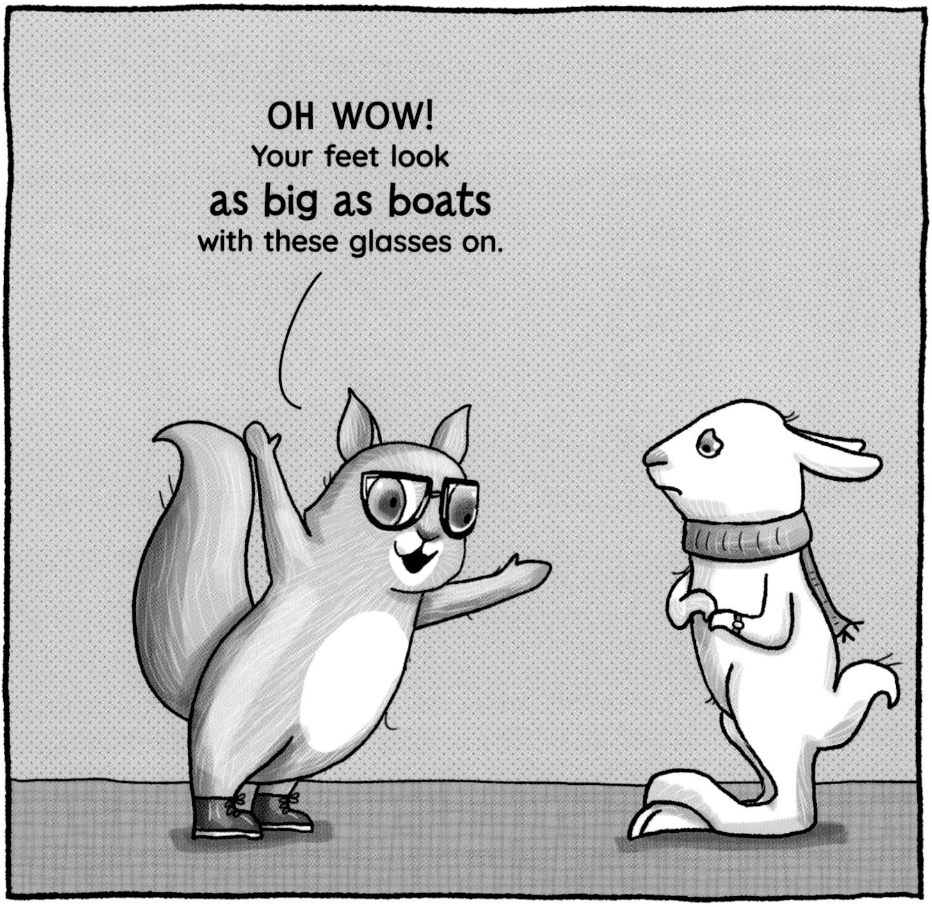
OH WOW!
Your feet look
as big as boats
with these glasses on.

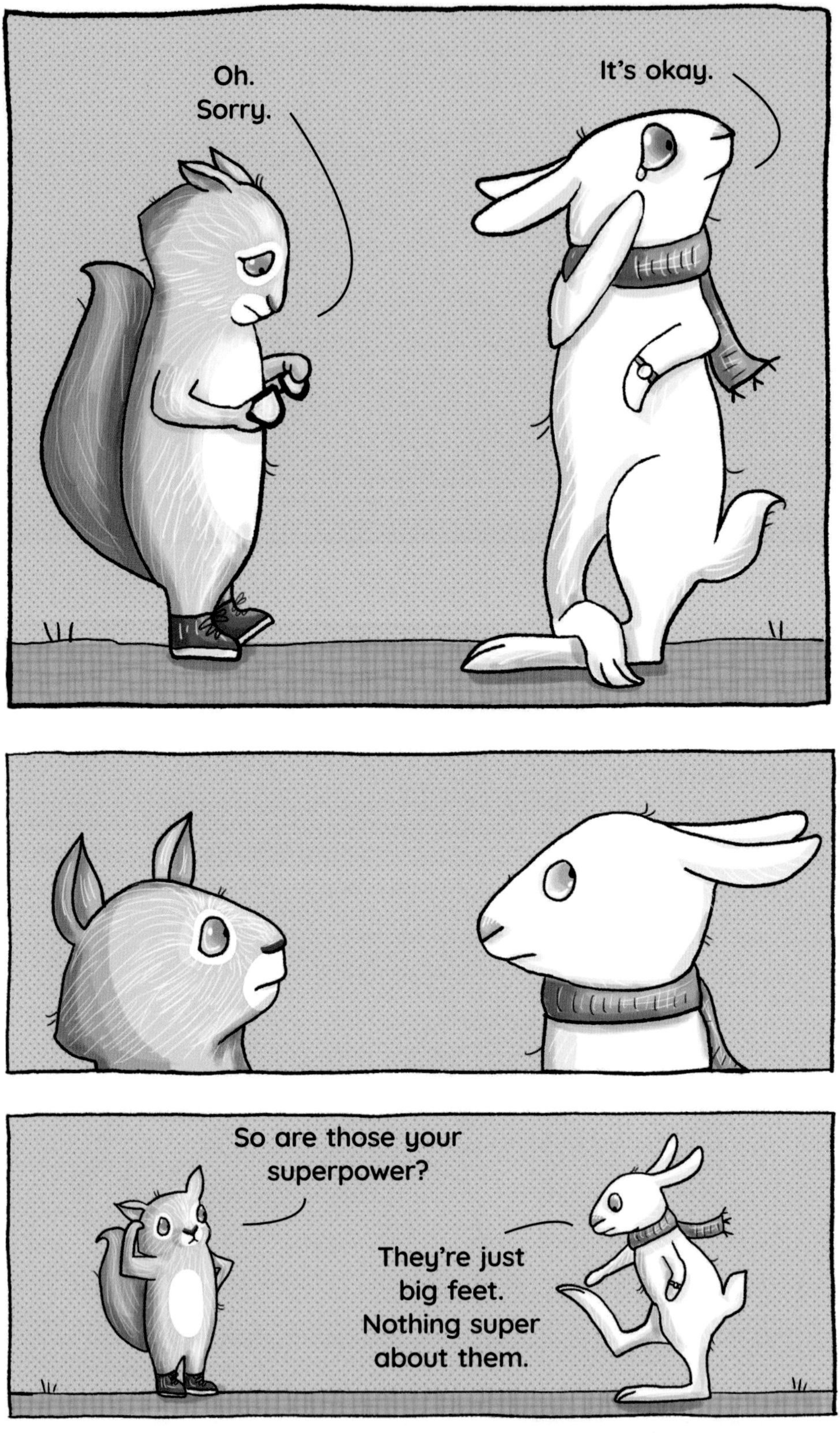
Oh.
Sorry.
It's okay.
So are those your superpower?
They're just big feet. Nothing super about them.

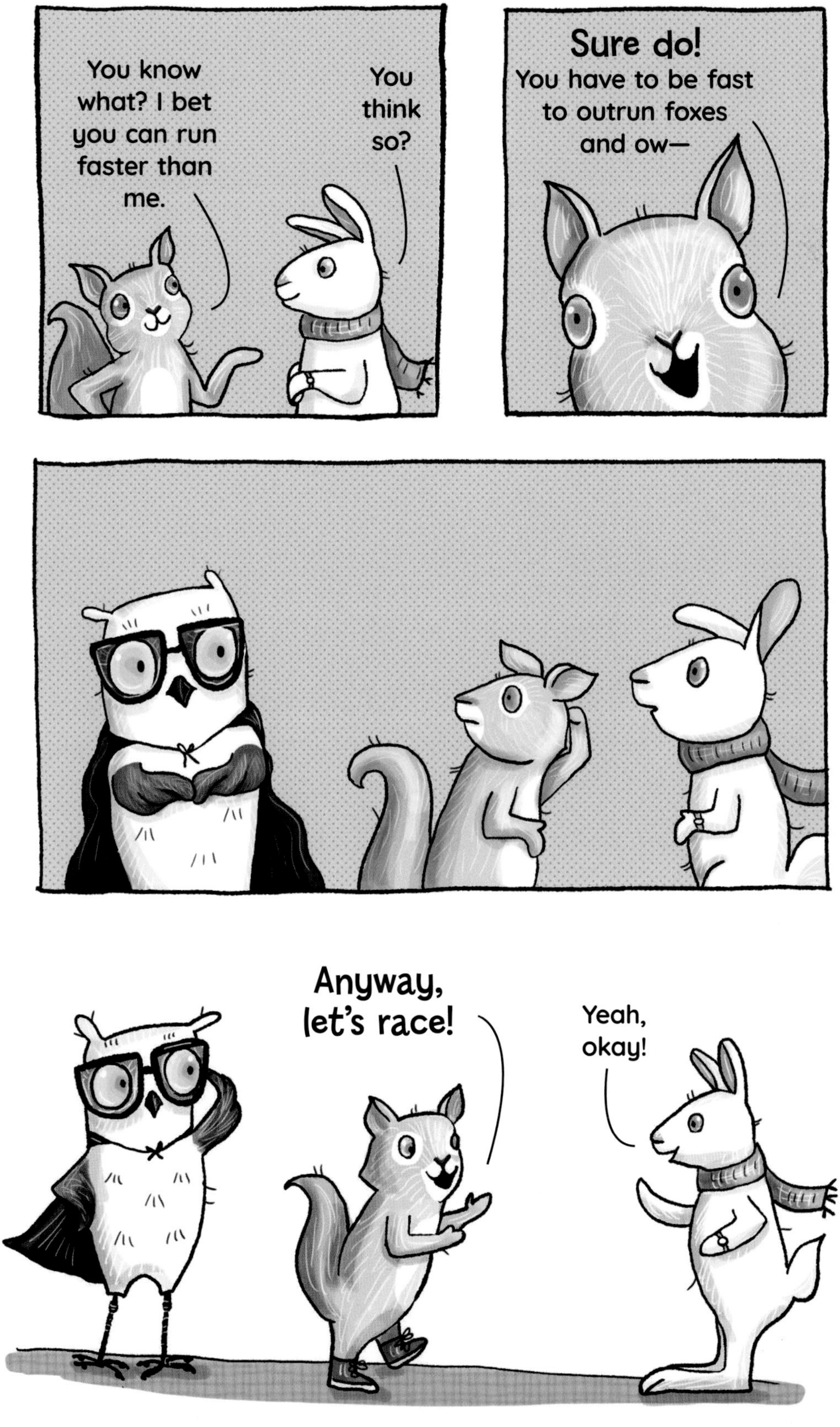
You know what? I bet you can run faster than me.
You think so?
Sure do!
You have to be fast to outrun foxes and ow—
Anyway, let's race!
Yeah, okay!

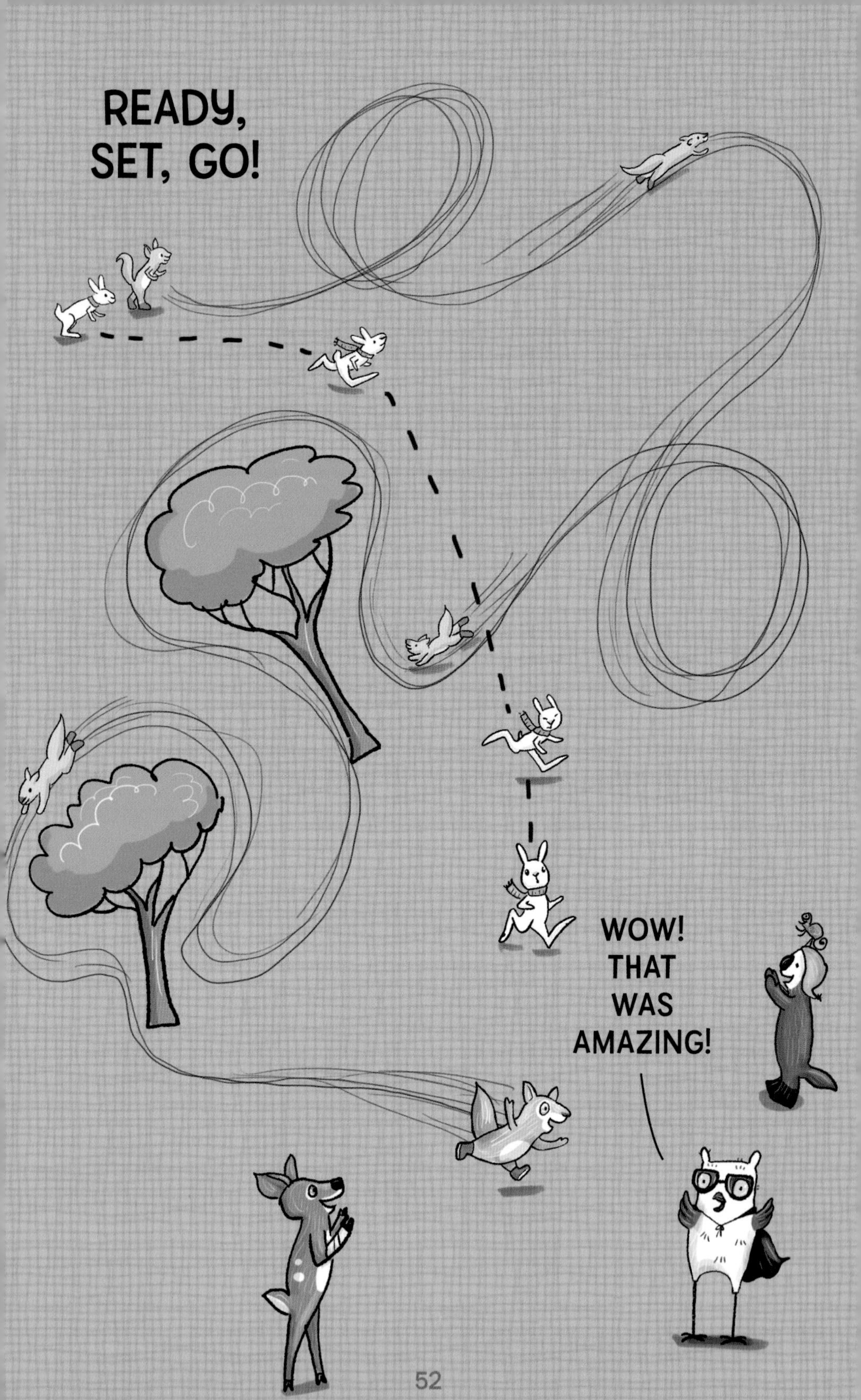
READY, SET, GO!
WOW! THAT WAS AMAZING!

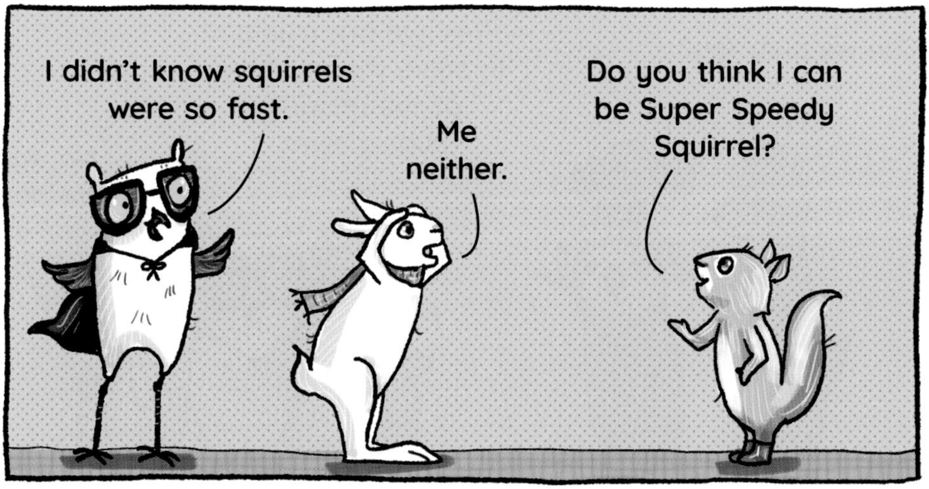
I didn't know squirrels were so fast.
Me neither.
Do you think I can be Super Speedy Squirrel?

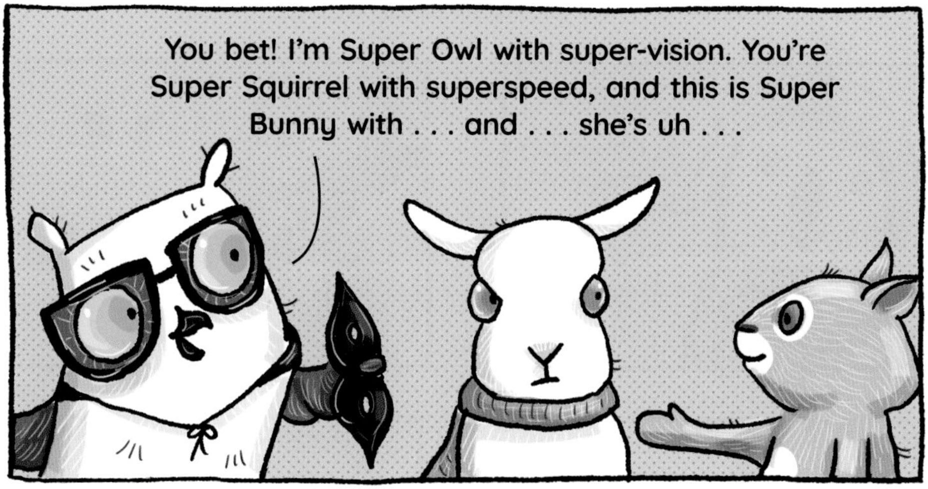
You bet! I'm Super Owl with super-vision. You're Super Squirrel with superspeed, and this is Super Bunny with . . . and . . . she's uh . . .

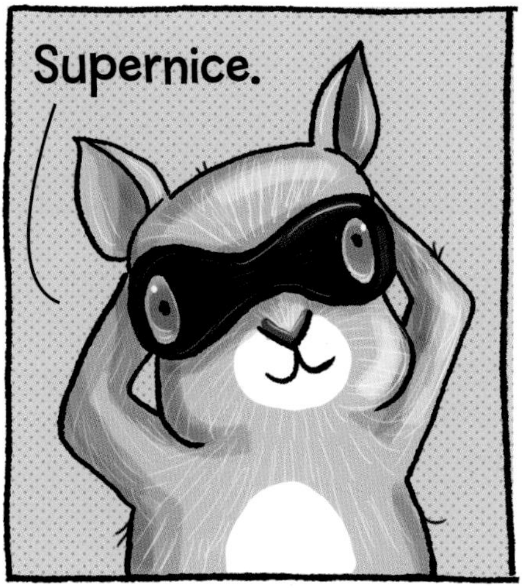
Supernice.

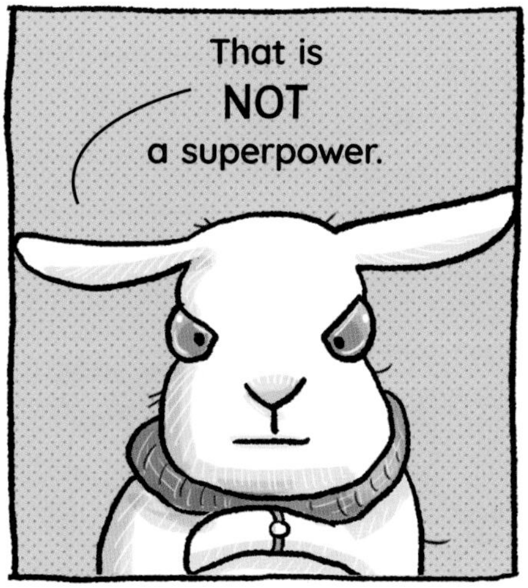
That is NOT a superpower.

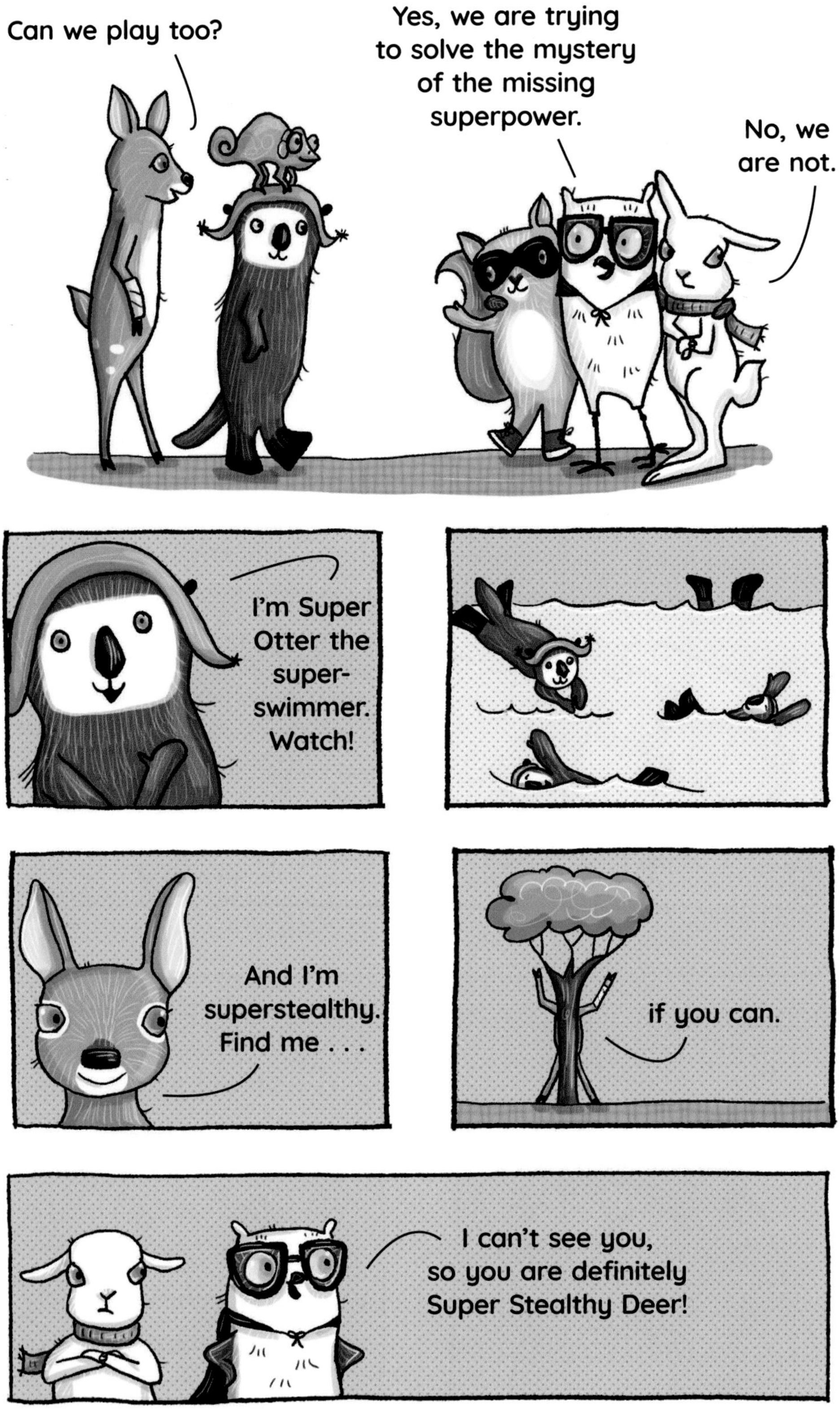
Can we play too?
Yes, we are trying to solve the mystery of the missing superpower.
No, we are not.
I'm Super Otter the super-swimmer. Watch!
And I'm superstealthy. Find me . . .
if you can.
I can't see you, so you are definitely Super Stealthy Deer!

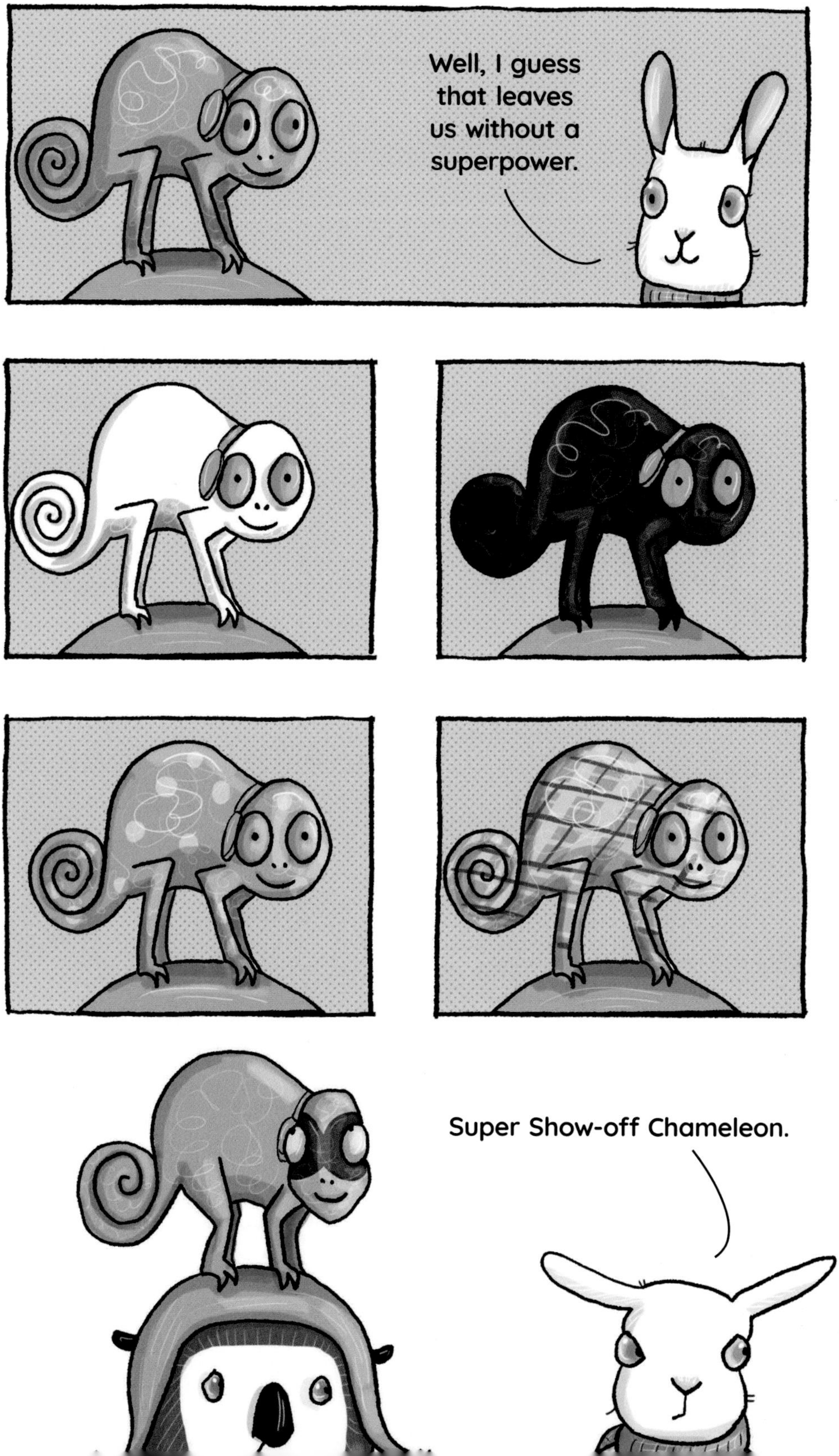
Well, I guess that leaves us without a superpower.
Super Show-off Chameleon.

CHAPTER 6

HOPPING MAD

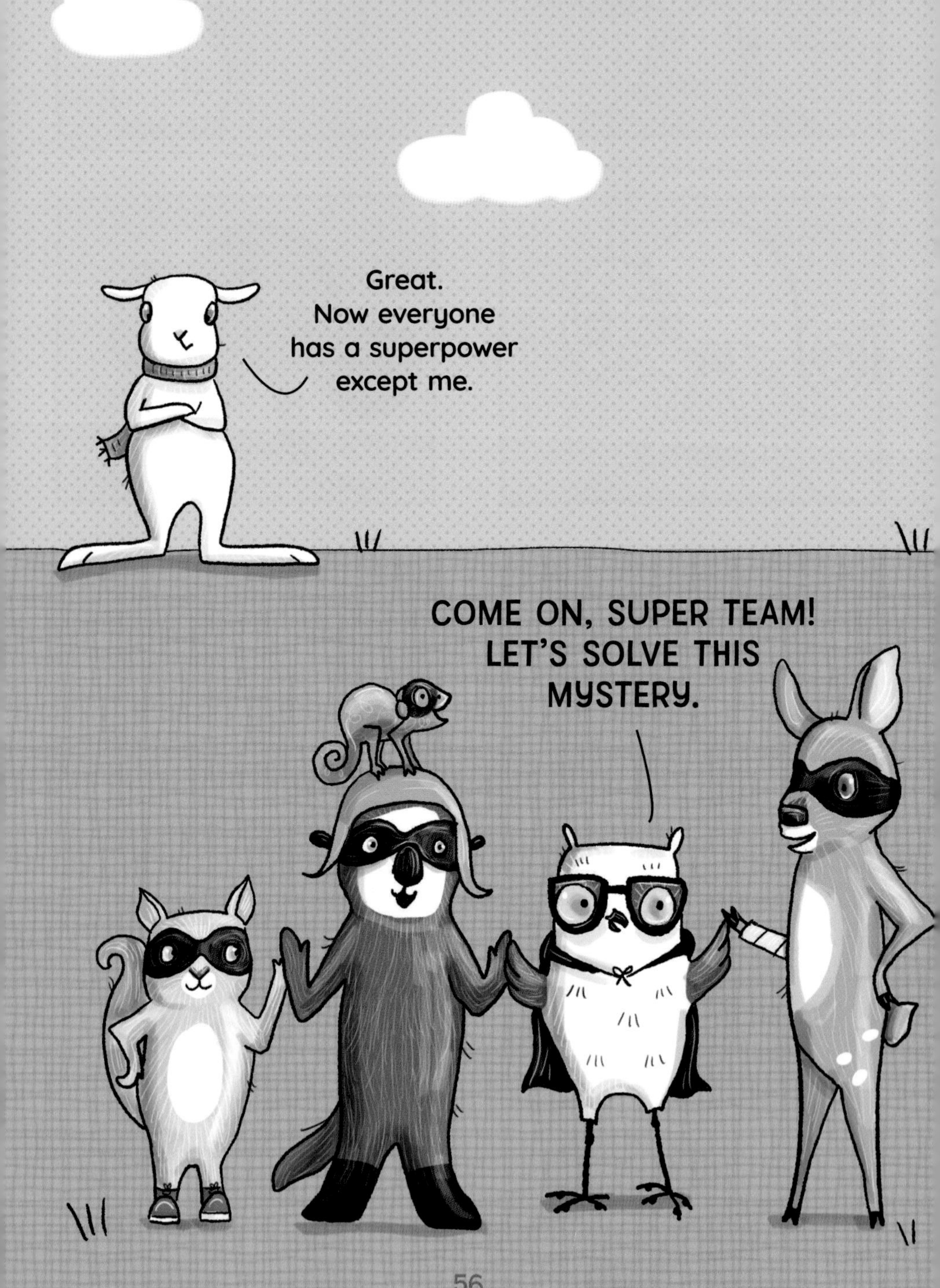
Great. Now everyone has a superpower except me.
COME ON, SUPER TEAM! LET'S SOLVE THIS MYSTERY.

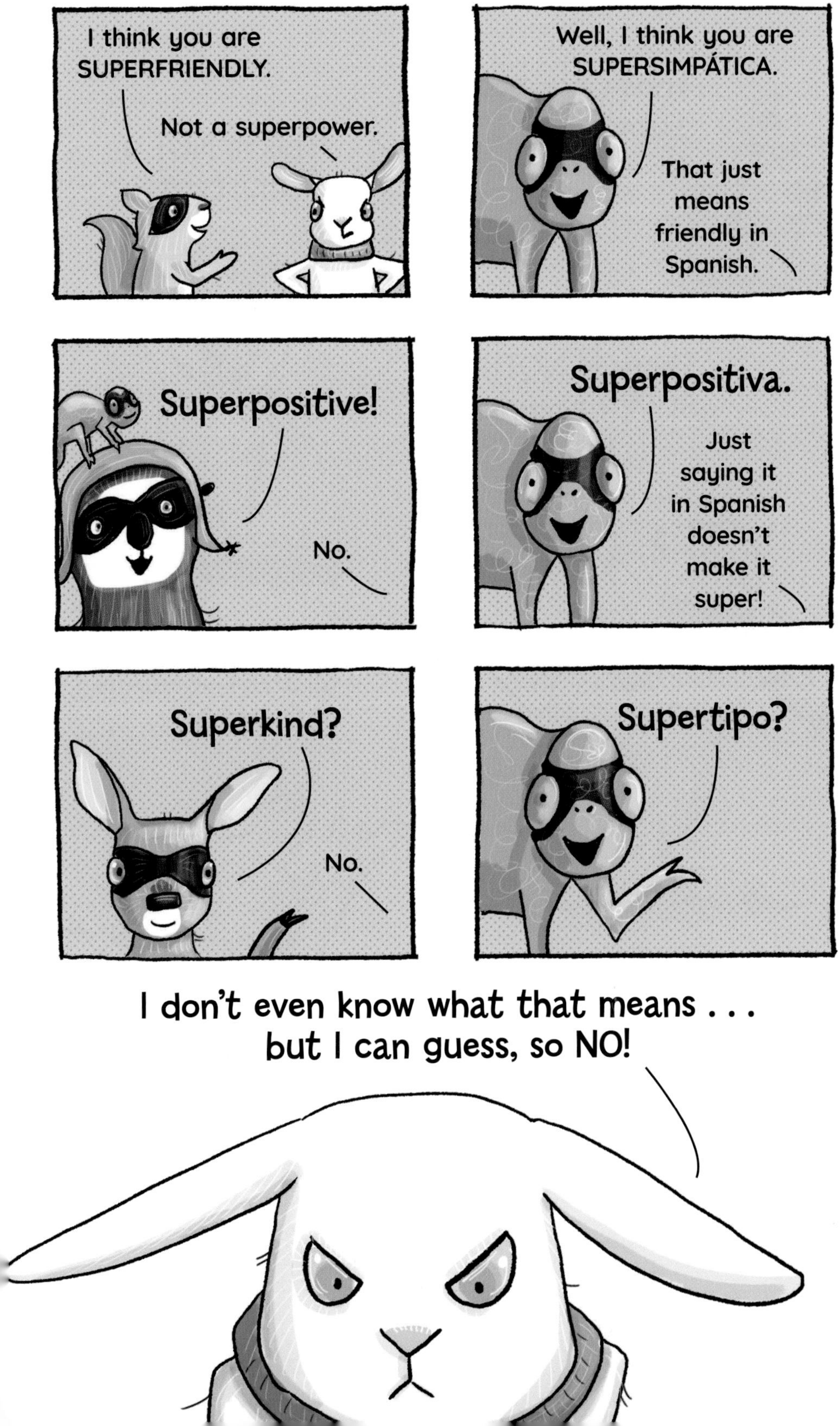
I think you are SUPERFRIENDLY.
Not a superpower.
Well, I think you are SUPERSIMPÁTICA.
That just means friendly in Spanish.
Superpositive!
No.
Superpositiva.
Just saying it in Spanish doesn't make it super!
Superkind?
No.
Supertipo?
I don't even know what that means . . . but I can guess, so NO!

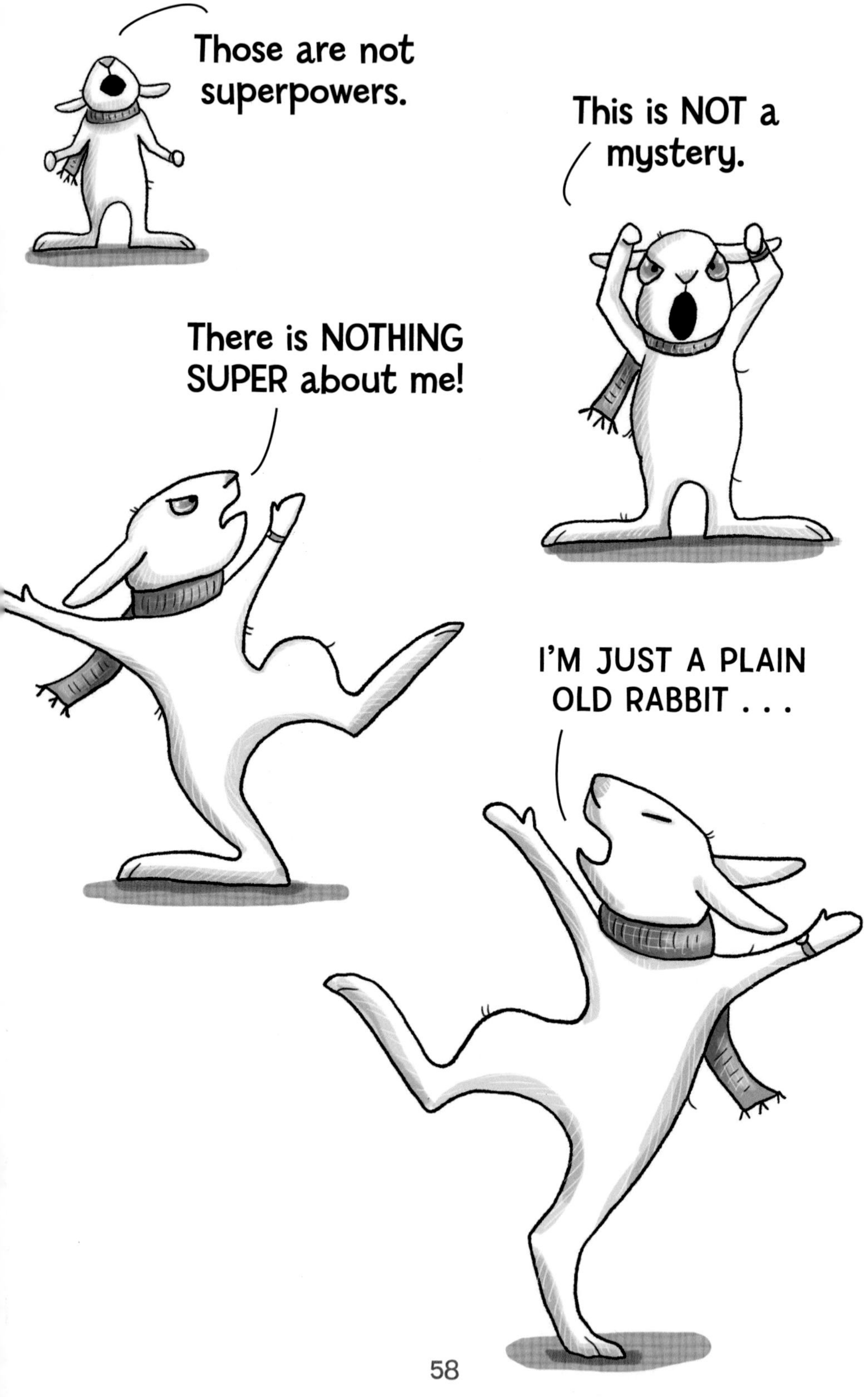
Those are not superpowers.
This is NOT a mystery.
There is NOTHING SUPER about me!
I'M JUST A PLAIN OLD RABBIT . . .

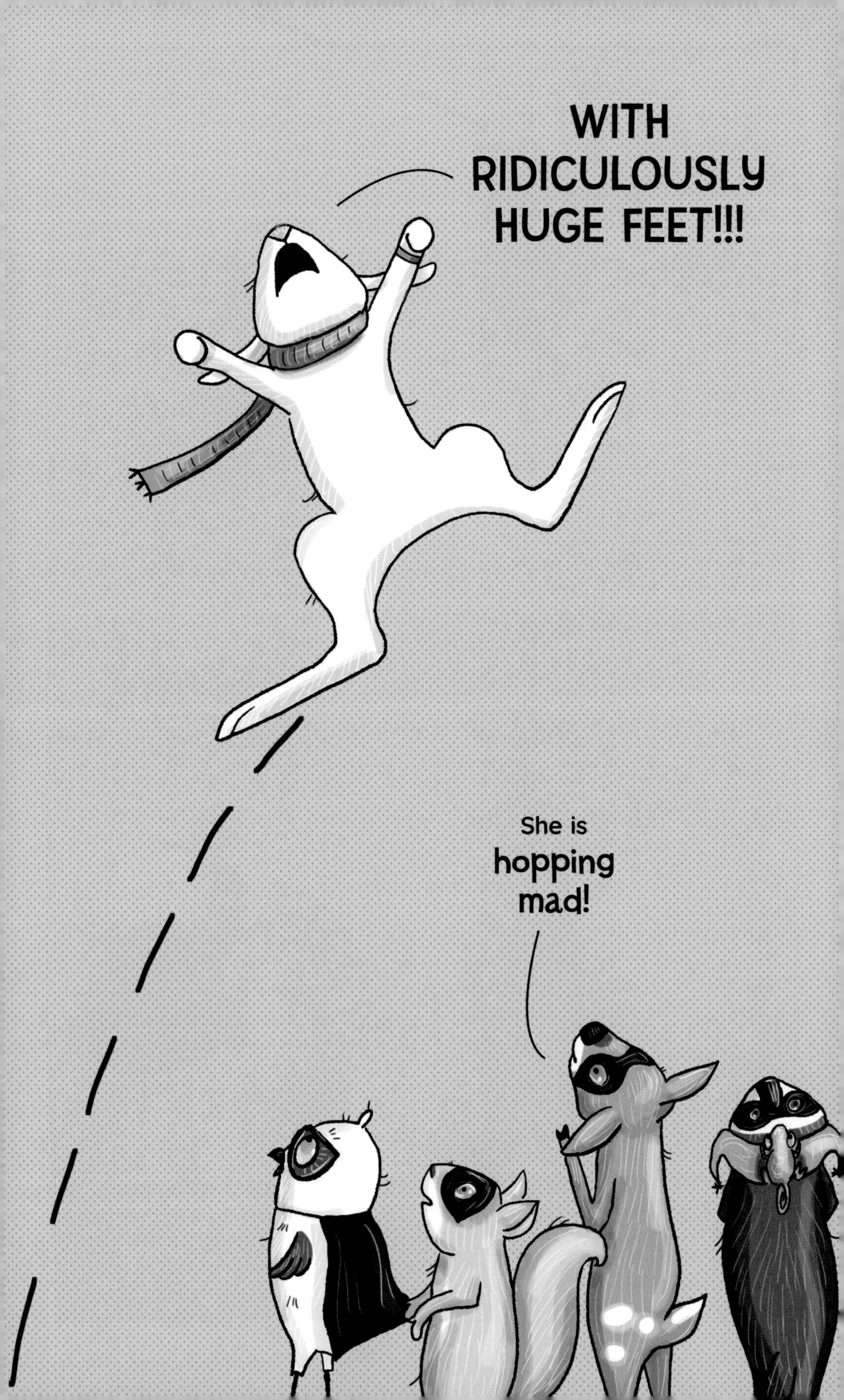
WITH RIDICULOUSLY HUGE FEET!!!
She is hopping mad!

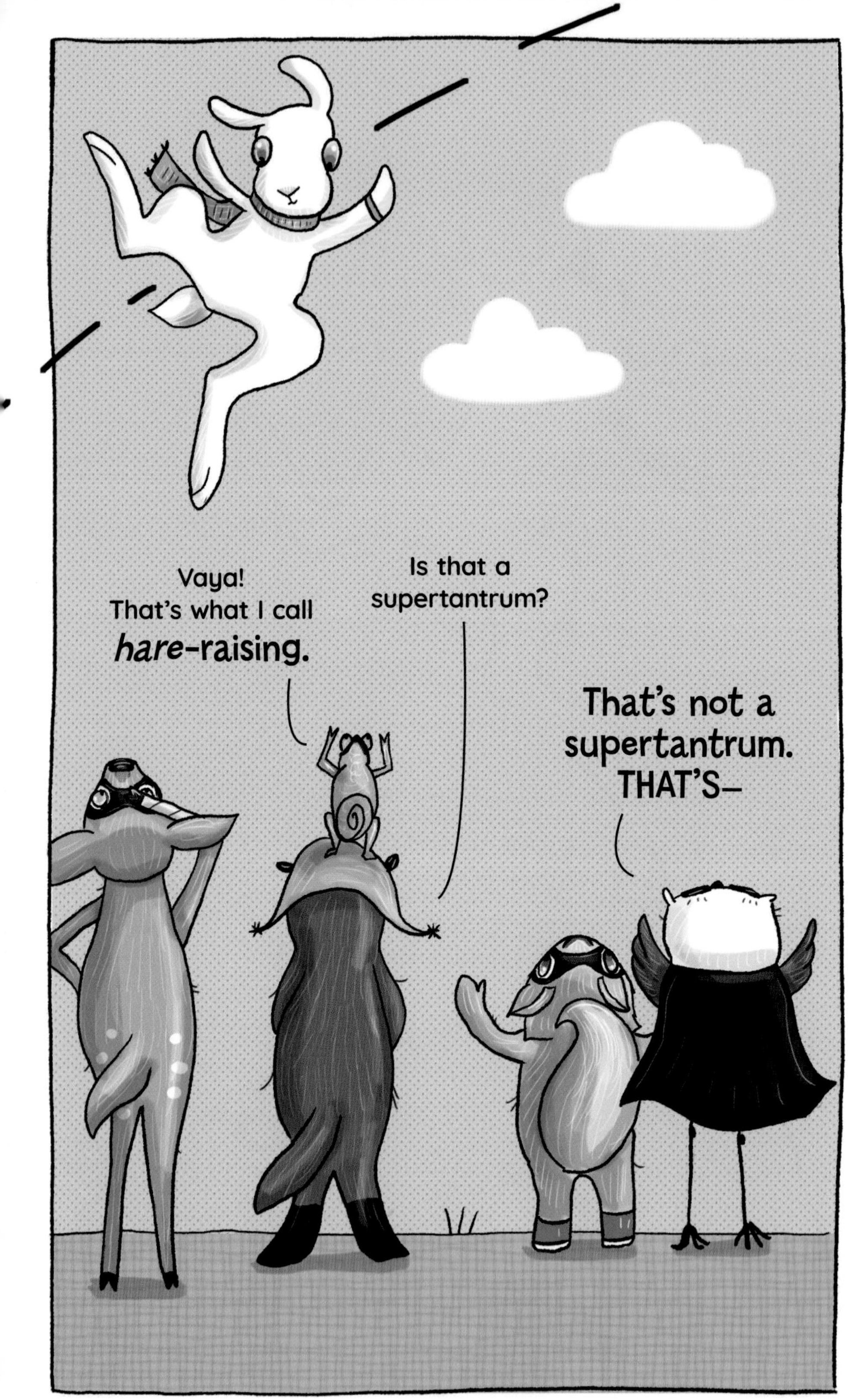
Vaya! That's what I call *hare*-raising.
Is that a supertantrum?
That's not a supertantrum. THAT'S–

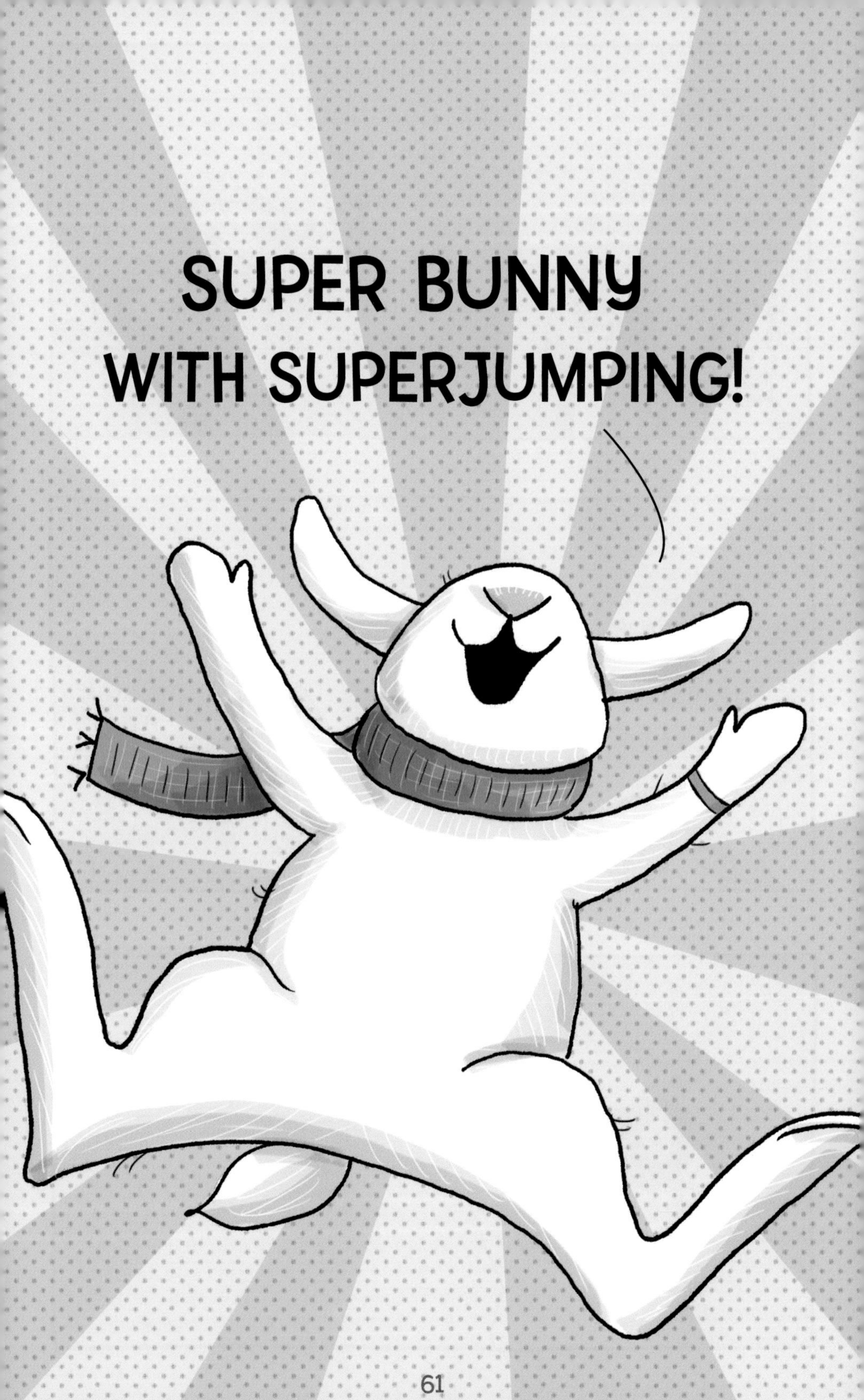
SUPER BUNNY
WITH SUPERJUMPING!

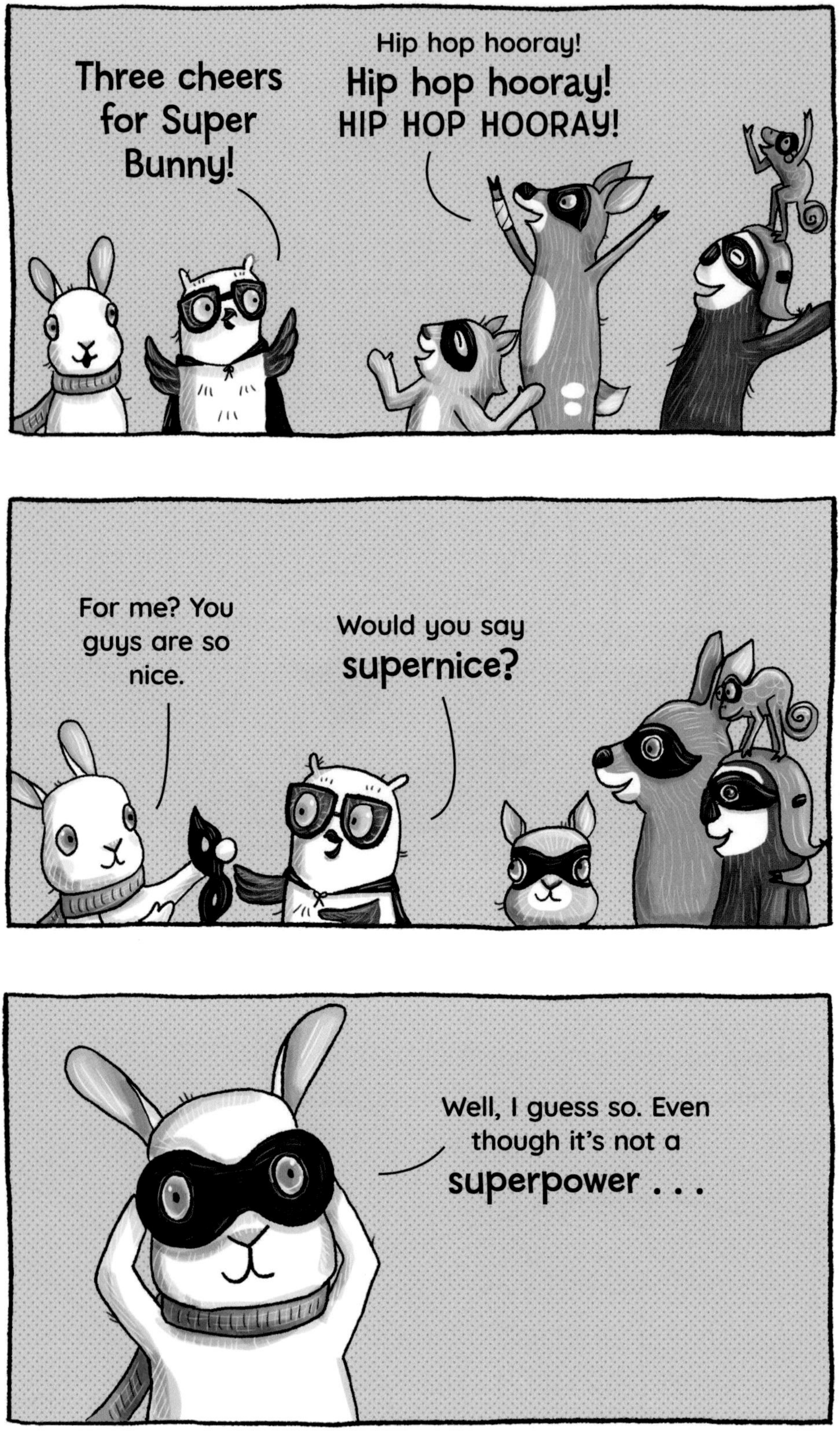
Three cheers for Super Bunny!
Hip hop hooray!
Hip hop hooray!
HIP HOP HOORAY!
For me? You guys are so nice.
Would you say supernice?
Well, I guess so. Even though it's not a superpower . . .

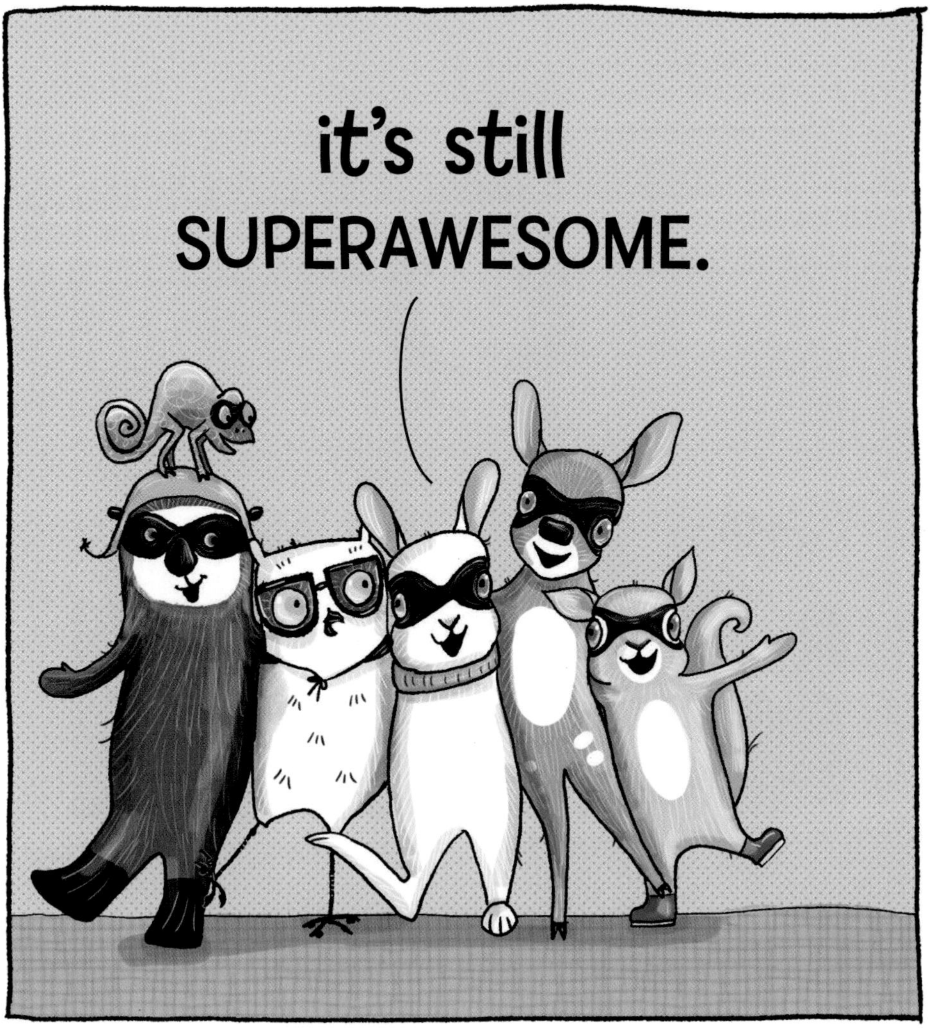
it's still
SUPERAWESOME.

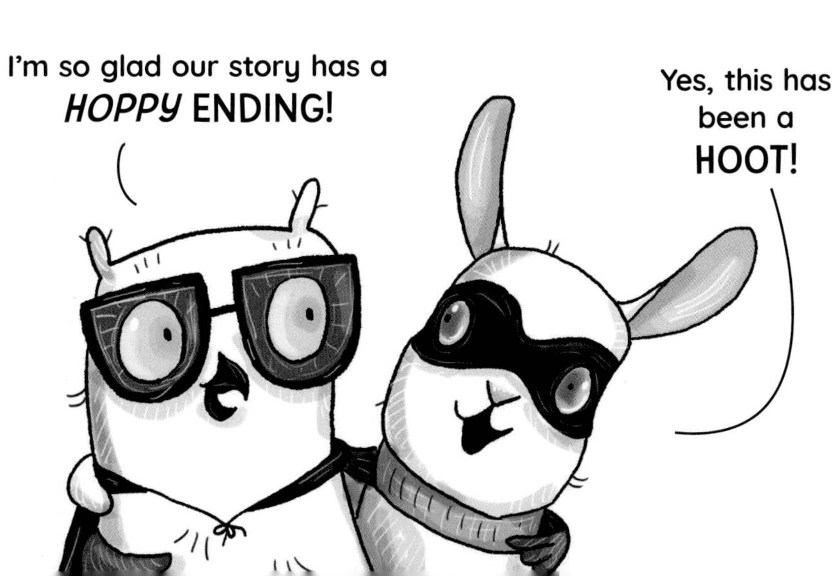
I'm so glad our story has a
HOPPY ENDING!
Yes, this has
been a
HOOT!

ABOUT THE CREATOR

Renée Treml was born and raised in the
United States and now lives on the beautiful Surf
Coast in Australia. Her stories and illustrations
are inspired by nature and influenced by her
background in environmental science. When
Renée is not writing or illustrating, she can be
found walking in the bush or on the beach, or
exploring museums, zoos, and aquariums with
her family and superenthusiastic little dog.